The Door in the Basement

Basement

By Josh Hilden

Publisher: Gorillas With Scissors Press

Literary Editor: Gypsy Heart Editing

Assistant Editor/Proof Reader: Jennifer Dembiczak

Book Formatting: Josh Hilden

Cover Designer: Gypsy Heart Editing

www.gwspress.net

www.joshhilden.com

Table of Contents

Chapter 1

"Unloading"

I didn't want to move to the farm. I mean, I liked visiting it when I was a kid during summer vacation, but I didn't want to *live* there. I was sad that Grandpa Roy was dead—we all were. But that didn't mean I wanted to uproot my life in Columbus and move to the middle of nowhere West Fucking Virginia.

But I couldn't tell Mom that.

She'd been devastated when word came that her father had died. Grandpa Roy had been changing a tire on the tractor when he had a heart attack. One of the farmhands found him half an hour later, but by then it'd been too late. When the will was read, the land, except for the house and four acres surrounding it, was sold off, and the money split between my aunts and uncles.

Mom inherited the house.

When Grandpa rewrote his will four years ago, Mom asked him if she could have the house instead of money. None of my aunts and uncles wanted the house. I think Grandpa was relieved and gratified to learn just how much Mom loved where she grew up.

"Alison, move your butt," Mom called from the back of the rental truck.

Since I'd turned sixteen in June, I'd driven the car here while Mom drove the Budget truck containing all our worldly possessions. I'd wanted to spend the last two weeks of summer vacation at the pool with my friends, but instead I'd been forced to participate in the move

Like I said, I was not happy.

"I'm coming," I yelled from inside the house. We'd been working fo over an hour moving boxes without a break. I was hot, tired, thirsty, and pissed off.

I stomped back out to the truck to see the pile of boxes Mom had staged for me to take inside. She was carrying several objects inside as well, so I couldn't bitch that she wasn't doing her part. Mom has never been a lazy person. Just because her job was one she could do from home didn't mean she was lazy. Mom worked hard as a technical writer and made sure we lived a good life. It'd been just the two of us since Dad didn't come home from Afghanistan.

I barely remember him.

I picked up one of the boxes Mom had stacked next to the truck. We'd labeled where everything went before leaving Columbus so there would be no guessing where to put it. In big, black Sharpie-drawn letters the word *'Basement'* was scrawled.

My heart nearly stopped. Long forgotten memories clawed at the back of my mind. They were cold, shadowy things covered in claws and fire that refused to clarify. My breath started coming in labored gasps. I felt small, young, and terrified. Something was forming, an image, a word, I almost had it…

"Alison," Mom yelled from behind me.

I nearly jumped out of my shoes.

"Look, Ally, I know you don't want to be here. I know you're mad that I made you move here. But this is my home, and this place is special to me. Please, honey, can you just help and stop fighting me?" she asked with grief in her voice.

"I'm sorry, Mama," I said, feeling like the petulant child I'd been.

"It's okay, Ally… maybe I should have tried to be a bit more understanding of your situation," she said.

I felt punched in the gut—Mom never admitted she was wrong. I picked up the box and smiled at her. "Can we take a break after we finish this pile?" I asked, indicating the stack of boxes .

"You know what, let's knock off when we finish it. Then we can head into town for some dinner," she said while running a hand through her damp hair.

"What about the rest of the stuff?" I asked. The idea of finishing after eating dinner did not appeal to me.

"Let it sit until tomorrow," she said, grinning. Then she picked up another box and headed back towards the house.

I felt pretty good when I turned back to the box marked *'Basement'*. It made me uneasy for some reason I still couldn't lay my hands on, but the feeling of terror I'd experienced before was gone.

Quit freaking yourself out.

I scooped the box up and headed toward the back of the house. The entrance to the basement was through a bulkhead. There was a door inside the house leading to the basement, but Grandpa never used it because he said the stairs were weak.

I approached the double bulkhead door and my vision went a little blurry. Just as I thought I should stop and use the inside door, my vision cleared.

I didn't like this at all.

I sat the box down, turned the handle, and opened the doors. There was a wet, earthy smell coming from the dark interior. I knew the basement was dry as a bone, but it still smelled wet. Reaching inside the doors, I flipped the modern light switch and the bright fluorescent lights illuminated the interior.

I don't want to do this.

Don't be stupid—it's just a basement. Take the damn box down there.

Grandpa said not to go down alone.

Grandpa didn't want you falling down the stairs when you were little.

I don't know...

Pull up your big girl britches and get down there!

I lifted the box and stepped down into the basement.

Chapter 2

"Into the Hatch"

The steps were concrete. I'd watched as Grandpa Roy and a few of his friends poured them over the course of a weekend. Once the custom blocks dried, they set them into place. Each step should have echoed off the steps and reverberated off the ancient masonry walls and corresponding concrete floor as they had every time I'd been down there as a child.

Each of my steps was silent.

The lights burned brightly in the space below me. It should have rendered the basement as bright as one of the grow rooms my Uncle Ralph grew his special strains of weed in, purely for medicinal purposes of course. I still felt like the void I was entering danced with dark unseen shadows.

Goosebumps exploded across my skin.

In the back of my mind, I knew this was a bad idea.

I took three steady steps down into the basement. My mouth and nose filled with a wet, moldy odor. I was painfully reminded of ditches filled with still water and rotting plants. I wanted to vomit. But there was no water in the basement.

The house was extremely watertight and with the valley being high in the mountains, the water table was more than two hundred feet below the property. Mom liked to tell me about when Grandpa had the artesian well drilled when she was little, and they no longer had to rely on the fickle river to supply their water.

But the smell of wet rot was making my eyes water.

A dozen steps more and my feet were on the textured red floor. Grandpa Roy had been determined to have a red floor even if he'd had to have the concrete dyed. He once told me he wanted to import red granite, but it'd been, "Too damned expensive, Ally," and he'd settled for the dye job.

The nearly brand new natural gas-fired furnace and water heater were down here along with the massive electrical panel that controlled the entire farm—these all dominated one wall. The longest wall of the "L" shaped basement was completely covered with floor to ceiling shelves. They were half filled with whatever Grandpa Roy had chosen to store down there.

Most men of Grandpa Roy's age would have installed some kind of workshop in the basement. But Grandpa had converted part of the old barn into a workshop. He refused to spend time in the basement if he didn't have to, yet he always kept it clean and secured.

I crossed the floor towards one of the empty shelves and shivered.

Of course, it should have been cooler in the basement. It was hot as hell outside, but a basement was an excellent thermal insulator, so it should have been very comfortable. It was almost cold enough to preserve meat in the basement. I could see wisps of breath emanating from my mouth. The sweat that had been covering my body quickly dried on my bare skin, leaving me painfully cold.

I sat the box on the solid shelf and turned to go.

That was when I saw the door open.

In the short section of the "L" shaped basement was the door leading up through the house. There was a door on all three floors (First, Second, and Attic) each of them heavy, dark honey-colored affairs. They were always kept locked. This one was different—it was the size of two doors, and it split down the middle to open like the doors of a barn. It was made of a dark, evil looking wood set in a brass frame. Brass hinges held it to the frame and bands of brass crossed each side of the door. Massive silver knobs set on plates with ancient looking keyholes completed the tableau.

I'd been in the basement once as a child. I don't remember what happened, and I don't know why I'd entered the room in the first place. But the next thing I knew I was sitting in the big chair, and Grandpa was giving me a cup of hot cocoa even though it was summer.

I spent the rest of the day trying to get warm.

The door now stood cracked open before me. The gap was just wide enough to allow a foot to enter. There was a pale purplish-red light glowing from behind the door. I could hear the sounds of air moving almost like someone or something was breathing. It reminded me of what a horse sounded like after it'd ridden farther and harder than it should have. It was a wet, labored breathing.

I began to walk towards the door... I wasn't even aware I was doing it.

I'd seen this light before. Was it when I was a child? I wasn't sure, but this all felt alien and familiar at the same time. In the back of my mind, I wondered why Grandpa wasn't coming down the steps to save me like he'd done before.

Alison... Come to us, Alison. Come and feel the light.

The voice was in my head. I wasn't hearing it with my ears. I heard it with my mind. I was scared and I wanted to stop and run back up the stairs. I knew I'd been here before and that Grandpa Roy had saved me. But there was nobody to save me this time. I was going to open the door... I was going to enter the light.

My bladder released.

My hand trembled over the knob.

"Alison, are you still down there?!" Mom yelled down the bulkhead hatch.

The spell broke and the door closed.

I ran up the stairs and back into the warm light of day.

I was freezing cold.

Chapter 3

"The New Town"

Mom was better than her word. We headed into the small city of Mason, West Virginia, with less than fifteen thousand residents, and had Thai food. It was really good, and that surprised me more than anything else about my new home. Even in the middle of the mountains you could still get good Pad Thai. I was starting to think maybe this place wouldn't be so bad.

I hadn't been to Mason since I was ten and it'd changed quite a bit.

"There has been a huge influx of tourism in the last few years," Mom said when she saw the surprised look on my face. "Your grandfather didn't normally like strangers in town, but when the roads were all resurfaced with the revenue from the visitors, he quit bitching."

I busted out laughing. That sounded so much like Grandpa Roy.

Dinner was excellent and the night was cool and dry. Mom asked if I just wanted to walk up and down Main Street and check out how much her hometown had changed. The positive energy of the town was amazing. After a massive hand dipped ice cream cone, all of the scary things that'd happened at the house were forgotten.

Mom had stopped to enter a shop specializing in homemade

pickles, jams, and jellies when I saw a store called Moon Dust. The storefront was clean with a simple but stunning sign over the main door. It was the combination pentacle and crescent moon in the window that ensnared me.

"Mom," I called out before she went into the jelly store. "I'm going across the street."

"Okay, Ally. Keep your phone on," she said, smiling at me.

When I walked into the shop, soft bells tinkled and the smell of lavender and incense filled my senses. Light music from some wind instrument played in the background. All of these things gave Moon Dust a very calm and safe feeling.

"Hello," a female voice said from the far counter. I looked across the dimly lit room and saw a tall, thin woman. She was maybe ten years older than me, and her pale skin was dotted with a spray of freckles. Her red and gold hair was pulled back with a gypsy style head wrap. She wasn't pretty in a conventional sense, but she was stunning in some indefinable way. "Welcome to Moon Dust. My name is Lydia."

"Hi, I'm Alison," I said, walking over to the counter.

She offered me her hand and I took it in my own.

My hand felt like I grabbed a live power cable after a thunderstorm. The feeling traveled up my arm and raced to every corner of my body. My body went rigid and my mind filled with images. I knew I was in pain but that was to the side.

I saw the door in my basement, it was open and the light was shining through the crack. I knew I was reliving something from my past but it was different from what'd happened earlier that day. The basement in my vision was darker and filled with a lot more junk. The floor was still the dirty flag stone mess it'd been before the red concrete was poured and even though I wasn't looking at them, I knew the steps behind me were the old wooden ones.

I was afraid, both versions of me were afraid. I could feel the fear in the Alison standing in Moon Dust and I could taste the terror of the Ally in the basement. I knew this was real, yet I couldn't actually remember it happening. I was reliving a forgotten memory.

Then the world went black.

"Are you okay," I heard the voice but was unable to open my eyes. "Oh please tell me you're okay, Alison," the shop woman was saying. I could tell by the closeness of her voice and my internal orientation that I was flat on my back and she was leaning over me.

The back of my head was in agony.

I opened my eyes.

"Oh thank the goddess," Lydia said when she saw my eyes open. "I tried to make it over the counter before you fell, but I wasn't fast enough. You should have been more careful and maybe asked before you touched my mind," she said, helping me sit up.

"What are you talking about?" I asked, drawing my knees to my chest while I waited for the room to stop spinning.

"When we shook hands you reached out and touched my mind,"

she said, looking me directly in the eyes. "You don't have any idea wha I'm talking about do you, Alison?" she asked.

"No," I said, my stomach finally settling and the weakness in my knees subsiding. My head was pounding. "Do you have any Tylenol?" I asked.

Lydia laughed softly. "Of course I do," she said, placing a warm hand on my shoulder.

I think I fell in love with her in that moment.

"Why don't you come in the back to my office—we need to talk," she said.

I was not offered a hand, not that I can say I blamed her, but she did wait until I was on my feet before heading into the back of the shop. We walked through gorgeously embroidered curtains into a cozy office and lounge area.

"What if you have a customer?" I asked, sitting on the very comfortable chair she indicated.

"I'll hear the bells," she said, smiling.

My heart melted a little.

She sat across from me and placed her hands on her knees. "Alison, we need to talk about your grandmother," she said with no lead up.

My jaw dropped open.

Chapter 4

"Grandma's Story Part 1"

"What do you know about my grandmother? For that matter, how do you know my grandmother? She's been dead since I was a little girl," I asked.

Lydia walked around the cozy room lighting candles. The room was filled with the smell of spices. There was a gracefulness to her movements I'd never seen outside of professional dancers. If I wasn't so freaked out about what'd happened in the front of the store, I would have been undressing her in my mind. As it was, I was at least enjoying the view.

"I didn't know your grandmother personally," Lydia said, sitting next to me on the comfy overstuffed loveseat. "She was part of the Moon Dust Coven long before I was born. She was one of the original seven sisters."

"I have absolutely no idea what you are talking about," I said, shaking my head in disbelief. Part of me really wanted to believe I was still passed out on the floor or better yet in an ambulance on my way to the hospital with major brain damage.

"There is a lot you don't know, Alison," she said and smiled sadly at me. "We've met before when we were both much younger. Do you remember the summer you stayed with your grandparents and you went into the basement?"

I was too stunned by the question to hesitate. "I didn't until today, but I've been... remembering things. I thought I was going crazy."

"You're not going crazy, Alison. Coming back here and moving into the old farm house has brought down the blocks my mother and your grandmother put in your mind," Lydia said. She looked like she wanted to take my hand in hers.

"How do you know all of this?" I whispered. Her words were scaring the hell out of me. Between what'd happened at the house, the incident in the show room, and now all of this information she had on me and my family, I just wanted to shut down. At that moment nothing sounded better to me than going back home and going to sleep.

Then I remembered that home was now the farmhouse on the hill.

"I grew up in the craft. Do you know what that is?" she asked me, raising an eyebrow.

"A bad movie from the 90s?" I replied, confused.

Lydia looked surprised then broke out into choking laughter. "Sorry," she said between gasps, "that was the last thing I would have guessed you'd say. Yes, it is a really bad movie, but I was referring to Wicca, do you know what that is?"

"Oh... yes I know what that is," I replied, flushing with embarrassment. I've never thought I'd be a girl to be flummoxed by a sexy voice and a pretty face, but there I was.

"Don't be embarrassed—your mother decided you should be kept out of the faith after she learned about what happened to you in the basement." Now she did take my hand and while there was a feeling of electricity when our flesh touched, like touching a nine volt battery to your tongue, there was none of the scary visions.

"My Mom knows about… it?" I asked, unable to articulate my fear of the basement and what I suspected dwelt there.

"Well," she said, looking away, "she knows but she doesn't want to know. Your mother left the circle when she met your father and moved away."

"Lydia, you're really confusing me," I replied, squeezing her hand.

When she squeezed back, I felt a jolt. Which was immediately followed by the fluttering of my heart. I want to be clear—I don't just crush on every girl I meet. I like to think I am pretty level headed. But this girl I'd just met had me acting like a lovesick idiot.

"I'm sorry, Ally. Let me start from the beginning."

Hearing my name out of her lips made me shudder inside.

Knock it the fuck off, Alison! I admonished myself. *This is serious, so stop imagining what her lips taste like!*

"Your family has owned the land you now live on for a long time," she said, drawing her legs up onto the couch and tucking them beneath her bottom. "I'm not sure who the first person to identify the darkness on the hill was. There are stories in the local native population going back into the mists of their antiquity about the evil trapped on your family's land." She hesitated before adding, "When you were little, it touched you."

I shivered at those words. The idea of doubting her never occurred to me. I knew she was telling me the truth. I'd felt the darkness behind the door. I knew in the deepest core of my soul this was not just a story... this was not a game.

"What's wrong, sweetie?" Lydia asked, looking at me with wide concerned eyes.

"I saw it again today," I whispered.

"Oh honey," she breathed, reaching forward and drawing me to her. Her hug was powerful. I felt some of my fear washed away and replaced with a warm feeling of safety.

"What is it?" I asked, embarrassed to realize I was crying.

"No one knows for sure, but your grandmother had a theory," she said, brushing a lock of my hair behind my ear.

"What?" I asked.

"I can't tell you—it'd be better if I showed you," she said, smiling.

"How are you going to do that? Did she record it?" I asked, confused.

"No silly," she giggled. "Give me your hands."

I hesitated.

"Trust me, Ally, I'd never hurt you," she said softly.

I slipped my shaking hands into her warm steady ones and fell down the rabbit hole.

Chapter 5

"Grandma's Story Part 2"

I was falling.

My body was still on the couch in Lydia's combination sitting room and office. I knew this but I also knew I was falling. My hands were still in Lydia's as the sensation of falling down a deep chasm consumed me. Yet I was also spread across a vast expanse of nothingness.

I was afraid.

Relax, Ally. Everything is all right, Lydia said. *I won't let you fall.*

It took me a second to realize her lips never moved. I was hearing her not with my ears but directly in my mind. This sparked a rapid flash of memories long sealed and kept under a psychic restraint. I saw myself as a little girl carrying on entire conversations with my grandmother, neither of us uttering a word. I saw myself at five years old playing with Grandma's cat Oscar and being able to hear his simple kitty desires. I knew in that moment something wonderful had been taken from me in order to protect me, and it filled me with alternating currents or anger and love.

Yes, Ally, I can see it all as well. I'm not trying to, but you've forgotten how to shield your thoughts. Right now you are a flashing beacon of images, Lydia thought to me.

All around us swirling mists of unformed thought danced and flashed. I considered what I'd been thinking about Lydia and both my mental and physical selves flushed a furious scarlet.

Did she know?

What was she thinking?

It's all right, Ally, everyone thinks things they don't want people to know. The thoughts you are embarrassed of are amazingly flattering, Lydia said into my mind, stopping for a second before continuing, *I think you are incredibly beautiful too.* She flushed too, but kept thinking at me. *When this is over I would love to take you out for a coffee. But right now we have serious things to deal with.*

Her words made me giddy.

Her words terrified me.

The endless falling through nothing ceased and Lydia began to guide us.

Where are we? I asked. I thought I knew but couldn't bring myself to accept it. I needed this woman whom I trusted with my life to confirm it for me.

We are inside your mind. I am taking you back to when you were little, she answered, sounding a little distracted as if she was concentrating very hard. *You are very strong, Ally. It's taking a lot of my talent to do this.*

I quieted to let her lead the way.

Moments in my life flashed by like images on a highway. I saw my first kiss, Rachael Anderson when I was twelve. Her mother had found out and made a stink, which was how I was outed. I saw the first time I drove a car. I saw a procession of birthdays and Christmases. I saw the day I realized my daddy was never coming home again. I saw the night before we moved when I got drunk with all my Columbus friends and ended up in bed with Jessica.

It was too much and I had to look away.

Almost there, Ally. Be strong, Lydia said as I felt bodies in the real world draw together and embrace.

Images clarified and the sensation of travelling stopped. We were standing side by side, hands held, in a very familiar setting.

We were in the basement.

I don't want to be here, I said, surprised to not hear my normal speaking voice but instead the voice of younger Alison.

I know, Lydia replied, *just remember, Ally, nothing here is real. This happened a long time ago and it can't hurt you more than it already has.*

I gripped her hand tighter.

We watched.

The bulkhead door of the basement opened and flooded the dark interior with light. I saw the stone floor and wooden steps. I knew what day this was. Inside I wanted to scream and break free of this, but I needed to know what'd happened that day.

Little Alison clicked on the single dim light and started down the steps. She wasn't trying to be bad. She had just wanted to see what was in the basement. She was irritated with Grandma for telling her it was off limits.

No, go back outside, I whispered, it even though I knew she couldn' hear me. My heart was hammering. I couldn't yet remember what came next, but I knew I was terrified.

She walked down the stairs and proceeded to inspect the boxes and crates stored in the dry cool space. She had her back to the recessed area where the door loomed, so she didn't see the light pulsating from the cracks.

RUN! I yelled, but of course little Ally couldn't hear me. This had already happened.

She opened a box marked 'X-MAS DECORATIONS' and began rummaging through it when the doors opened wide enough to allow a shaft of dark light to escape. I don't know why I thought of it as dark, objectively it was a yellowish white light. But it seemed to make everything darker despite the increased illumination.

Little Ally kept rooting through the box.

Please go back to Grandma, I begged the younger version of myself to no avail. I remembered what came next.

I could feel Lydia hugging me tight.

"Alison," a cold wet voice whispered from behind the door.

Icy chills filled my belly.

"Who said that?" little me asked, turning and seeing the light coming from the door for the first time. She dropped the ornate glass angel she'd been admiring and began walking wordlessly to the door.

The angel smashed on the floor.

A single green black tentacle slithered out from between the parted doors.

Oh my God, Ally, run away! my mind screamed at the girl.

She couldn't hear me.

The tentacle reached for her and instead of pulling away she lifted her hand to meet it half way. The slimy horror wrapped delicately around little Ally's wrist and in that moment I remembered all of it.

I remembered the pain.

I remembered the terror.

I remembered fighting for my life.

I remembered what Grandma did to save me.

But more than anything else, I remembered what was behind the doors in the basement.

Chapter 6

"Grandma's Story Part 3"

I was screaming inside my own head.

In the real world, I was shaking and convulsing on Lydia's well sprung love seat. In my mind, I was curled up on the floor of my grandparent's basement, shrieking in terror as my past self also shrieked. She was screaming for our grandmother and I was begging for my mother to come save me.

Ally, it's not real, Lydia said, dropping to the ground next to me. In the real world, her hands grasped mine tighter.

Sweetie, this happened a long time ago. It can't hurt you now. Ally, you need to see this, she pleaded with me.

I heard her and I wanted to follow her lead, but I knew what I'd see. The dams were down and the past was flooding the memory centers of my brain. I was seizing up and locking down for my own safety.

Pain shot through my astral form when Lydia's mental self smacked me hard across the face. In the real world, my convulsions subsided, but in my mind I experienced a moment of perfect calm.

I turned and looked.

The tentacle dragged little Alison towards the gaping maw of the doors. She fought it. I was retroactively proud of her for fighting so hard when grown adults would have surrendered to the horror. She screamed for help and slammed her small hands into the tentacle.

I remembered the cold greasiness of it.

She's about to see it, I whispered.

Lydia moved closer to me and took my hand in hers. She was warm and filled me with a sense of safety and comfort.

Little Alison tilted her head up from the tentacle and looked into the light pulsating from behind the door. Once her eyes were trained on it, she stopped fighting and seemed to drift into some form of catatonia. But I remembered this, she wasn't in a catatonic state, she was hypnotized by the thing on the other side. In her mind, little Alison was aware and screaming for help.

It was those screams, not the verbal ones, that saved her life.

Just as little Alison's foot began to slip past the threshold and disappear into the light, the basement bulkhead doors flew open. Lydia and I turned to see my grandmother bolting down the stairs two at a time. She was like a goddess, her long honey colored hair whipped around her head like a halo and I knew what was about to happen.

Get it, Gran! I hissed, squeezing Lydia's hand so hard that if we were in our physical bodies I would have feared hurting her.

Gran was surrounded by a bright yellow light. I knew I was seeing a manifestation of her powers and I knew I'd seen it then as well. There was so much about the past I'd forgotten.

"You let her go!" Gran yelled. I could feel the power she exuded even in this memory. She was a living battery of energy.

The thing quit pulling on little Alison as sounds were emitted from beyond the doors. I think they were words, but the language and sounds were nothing ever spoken willing by a human. The sounds made the fillings in my teeth hurt, and my physical body vomited onto Lydia's carpet.

"You can't have her!" Gran yelled. A jet of liquid energy leapt from Gran's body and entered the opening.

The thing yelled in rage and pain.

Little Alison began sliding into the light beyond the threshold once more.

"No!" Gran screamed, charging towards her and grabbed hold of her wrists. The older woman pulled and her bright yellow energy flowed across little Alison's body.

The thing roared.

I clapped my hands over my ears. That was when I realized the cry was not audible, it was in my mind. I looked at Lydia and saw a look of agony on her face. She was hearing it as much as I was.

The tentacle retreated and Gran gathered little Alison into her arms.

The massive doors slammed shut.

I think it's time to go, Lydia said as Gran closed the bulkhead door.

No, I responded. I knew what was coming next. I remembered it and I knew Lydia might not believe it if she didn't see and hear it for herself. I'd been there and I was having a hard time believing it even now.

We followed Gran up the stairs. We passed through the bulkhead and out onto the sunlit grass. Gran was sitting on the ground and had little Alison lying on her lap.

"Everything will be okay, Ally," Gran cooed, rocking her and humming.

I wrapped an arm around Lydia's waist. I needed her support because I was feeling an almost irresistible urge to run away. She wrapped her arms around me and drew me close.

On the ground, little Alison began to convulse.

"Roy!" Gran screamed, never taking her eyes off of my younger self.

I knew Grandpa would come, but not until after it happened.

What's happening? Lydia whispered, holding me tighter.

Be brave, love, it'll be over in a minute, I said, the rolls were flipped I was leading and she was following.

Little Alison stopped thrashing and went as rigid as a board. Then she began to speak. The voice was one of a woman much older than I am, closer to that of my Gran than to me. There was a haunting echoing quality to the words.

"The dweller is returning and the cracks between the worlds grow wider. The gates to The City of the Dark Light have been opened once more. Great armies are on the move and the Old Ones have turned their eyes toward the world of humans."

I remembered this. I knew she could see me. I knew she was talking to me. Terror filled my abdomen and my heart pounded beneath my breasts.

"You must close the crack. The dweller must be caged once more. Do this or all you know and love will end and we will all be meat for the beasts."

Before I could reply, I felt myself be dragged back up towards consciousness. Lydia and I ascended back to reality, leaving the events of my past behind.

Chapter 7

"Waking Up"

I snapped back to consciousness, the words of warning fresh on my lips. The smell of my half digested dinner filled the room and I was shocked to realize I was lying half on the couch and half on the floor. Every joint and muscle in my body screamed for relief.

"Ally, are you okay?" I heard Lydia ask from somewhere else in the room. She sounded shaky but in better shape than I felt. She continued speaking despite my lack of response, "I'm sorry I freaked out at the end, but that thing felt so... wrong."

"It's okay," I croaked, fighting to right myself. "If I hadn't remembered the first time I heard it, you would have been forced to catch me when I ran away."

I felt Lydia's hands slip around me and help me into a sitting position. Despite the warmth in the room, my bones were chilled and I began to shiver uncontrollably. It took a second for my addled mind to realize Lydia was shivering as well. I watched, half paralyzed, as she limped to a pile of blankets and took an ancient looking quilt off the top.

"What we did takes a lot out of someone on the best of days—this was not the best of days. We need to share body heat or we'll go into shock," her teeth chattered and her hands shook as she spoke.

Watching her do everything she could to help me... I knew I was falling for her in a bad way. This could be difficult, but for the moment I put it aside and was just grateful she was going to try and warm us. She wrapped the blanket around my shoulders, sat next to me, and enveloped us in a thick cocoon. We shook and wrapped our arms around one another.

"What was that thing?" Lydia asked once we'd begun to reach a livable, if not comfortable body temperature. "My mom never said what was down there, just that it was bad. If I'd have known ahead of time..."

"You did brilliantly," I said, pulling her tighter to me. She smelled really good and I fought the almost insane urge to kiss her. I needed to remind myself I'd just met her. But we'd been connected on a level I never imagined existed. It was all very confusing. I had no idea what to do.

Lydia cleared the confusion.

She turned her face to me and pressed her mouth to mine.

Our lips parted and our tongues traced one another's. It wasn't a forceful kiss, but it was a damn sexy one. Electricity jumped between us, and I don't mean that in some Harlequin bullshit way. I mean it felt like I was making out with a live wire but instead of pain it was pleasure. Well there was some pain but it made the pleasure even more intense. I'm sixteen not twelve—I've made out with plenty of girls and I'm far from a virgin but I'd never felt anything like this in my entire life. I could feel what it felt like for Lydia to kiss me as I was kissing her.

We broke apart and stared at each other with wide eyes. My lips were quivering and my heart was racing. I wanted her to throw me down on the couch and just get to it. But the rational part on me, damn that it even exists, knew better.

"Wow," I whispered.

We both jumped and a squeak escaped my lips when my phone began to ring. The sounds of the My Little Pony theme song filled the room and my face exploded in an embarrassed blush.

Why did she have to hear that? Why didn't I change my damn ringtone to something less childish? my mind screamed. Looking down, I saw my mom's face on the screen and out loud I said, "Sorry, I have to get this." Then I realized she might have heard the unspoken words.

"I like that show too," she said with a grin.

"Hi Mom," I answered.

"Where are you, sweetie?" Mom asked, sounding relaxed and happy. I had to remember that from her perspective we'd just had a wonderful dinner and some fun window-shopping. "I'm getting kinda tired."

"I'm still across the street at Moon Dust. Where do you want to meet?" I asked. I noticed the look on Lydia's face too late.

Mom said nothing but I could feel the change in atmosphere.

"Mom, what's wrong?" I asked hesitantly.

Lydia took my hand and I squeezed it reflexively. I could hear her in my mind. It was a little scary how used to it I was getting.

Don't be defensive, Ally. She didn't like my mom and was pretty mad at your gran after what happened to you that day. I don't know exactly what happened between them afterwards, but I know it was serious.

I could feel the love behind the thoughts and a calming warmness filled me. I think that was when I knew I would never want to live life without Lydia.

I knew she could hear those thoughts too.

"Why are you there, Alison?" Mom asked. There was something in her voice I'd never heard before and it took me a heartbeat to identify it. My mother was terrified.

"I just wandered in," I replied lamely. Mom has always been able to tell when I am lying and it dawned on me there might be a reason for that beyond her being one of the smartest people I knew. I knew as soon as I thought it that Mom was just like me.

"Stay there. I'm coming to get you," Mom said.

I spoke before she could hang up.

"How long have you known, Mom?" I asked, surprised to realize I was on the verge of tears.

Lydia scooted closer and wrapped her arms around me.

Mom sighed loudly before answering, "Since before you were born, Ally."

Chapter 8

"Mom Arrives"

"I don't want her in here, Lydia," I said, walking back and forth in the front area of the shop.

I didn't know why I felt this way. My mom had always been awesome—we were a team. It'd been us against the world. But the way she sounded on the other end of the phone scared me. That wasn't my mother. She may have been a close relative to her, but this person was a stranger to me.

"Your mother loves you, Ally—you know that," Lydia said. She was sitting on the stool behind her sales counter watching me pace the floor. Somehow she'd known that when I was agitated the last thing I wanted was a person trying hold and comfort me. "We're probably going to have an intense conversation when she gets here, but she does love you."

Her words had a calming effect on me, but I was so ramped up the effect was minimal. I'd seen my mother mad. I'd seen my mother scared. I'd seen my mother in the depths of sadness, but the feeling I'd gotten from her dwarfed all of those put together.

The bells over the door jangled.

I turned and saw her.

I think maybe it was the first time in my entire life I'd actually seen Rebecca Marie Mills. My experiences with Lydia had managed to reawaken senses I'd suppressed for years and what I saw was glorious. My mother, all five feet two inches of her, was surrounded in a swirling corona of white and blue light rising into the ceiling.

She was so powerful.

She was so glorious.

"Mom!" I said, all of fear melting away. I rushed to her and threw my arms around her. I'm nearly six feet tall and I've always assumed my father was descended from giants. She never even budged when I collided with her. I buried my face in her shoulder and sobbed.

"I'm so sorry, Ally. I just hoped this would pass you by," she said, sounding choked and fearful.

We held one another for several minutes before Mom broke our embrace and looked up at me. She was smiling and her eyes glistened with tears. She reached up and touched my face. Then I heard her in my mind.

I've wanted to tell you for so long how beautiful your light is.

What are you talking about? I don't have a light, I responded, confused.

Are you kidding? You shine like a star, Lydia said, joining out conversation. *I've never seen anything like it in my life.*

"Hello, Lydia," Mom said, dropping back to audible speech, a sad smile on her face. "I was so sorry to hear about your mother."

"Thank you, Becky. Mom never blamed you for leaving... You know that, right?" Lydia asked, looking concerned.

"Yes, but that makes me feel worse. Kelly was my best friend in school and when things got rough, I ran."

I was surprised to hear that. Mom never talked about her childhood unless she was telling stories about Gran and Grandpa Roy. The fact that my mom and Lydia's mom had been best friends gave me a surreal feeling of fate and destiny.

Lydia stepped out from behind the counter and joined us. Without thinking about it, I slipped my hand in hers and squeezed. Mom saw and raised an eyebrow at us. I saw the familiar face of Mom in protective mode, and then she softened.

"Do I even need to tell you if you hurt her I'll make you sorry?" she asked Lydia, giving her a lopsided, sad smile.

"No ma'am," Lydia replied, pushing closer to my side.

"How long have you known?" I asked, feeling more uncomfortable about this point than anything else that had transpired today.

"I've always known," she said and now she looked tickled. "Every time you saw a girl you thought was cute your aura spiked a bright orange. It's just who you are sweetie, which is all that matters to me."

I smiled.

"But we need to have a talk," Mom said, her face hardening. "Is the back room still comfortable, Lydia?" she asked.

"Yep, as long as you don't mind the smell of vomit," she said, squeezing my hand again.

"I've smelled worse and we need a bit of privacy," Mom said, walking behind the counter and entering the back room.

I wrapped my arms around Lydia and held her tight. "I thought she was going to be so mad at me. Then she walked in here and it was like a goddess had come down from Olympus," I knew I was babbling, but I didn't care. I was overwhelmed by the intensity of her arrival.

"I don't think it's safe to say she's happy about all of this," Lydia replied, stroking my hair.

This was crazy, I knew it was crazy, but we'd been deep in each other's minds. We'd tasted our hearts and found them in synch with one another.

"I know what you're thinking and I'm thinking it too," she said before kissing me on my cheek, and then she took my face in her hands and looked at me. "I love you. I know that sounds insane but I do. I feel like I've known you all of my life."

I kissed her full on the lips before she could say anything else.

"If you two are done, there is a lot we need to do and it's been a long time since I've done any of it," my mom called from the back room.

We broke our kiss and giggled like children.

"I love you too," I said once the giggles subsided.

Holding hands tightly, we headed behind the counter and into the back room. I had no idea what might happen next, but I had my mother and the woman I loved by my side. I was ready for everything.

At least I thought I was.

Chapter 9

"The Past is Prologue"

"There is another world side by side with the one we know and experience every day," Mom said with no preamble. "I think you've already realized that, but I just want you to understand it's a fact not a fairy tale."

I was sitting back on the sofa, my side pressed firmly against Lydia's. Part of me wanted to hear everything my mother had to say but the other part of me, the little girl who'd barely escaped that basement so many years before, wanted it all to go away. I was getting agitated and a bubble of terror was blossoming in my gut once more. Lydia must have known what I was thinking because she slipped her hand in mine and squeezed. Strength and warmth flowed from her to me.

I calmed and listened to my mom who was still talking.

"I'm a witch, your gran was a witch, her mom was a witch," Mom continued. "I think you can see where I'm going with this."

I nodded solemnly, but suspecting something and knowing it for certain were two very different things. I was afraid to ask the obvious question, and thankfully Mom spared me the effort.

"You're a witch too, Ally," she said sadly.

"What does that mean?" I finally asked. "Does it mean I'm evil?

Does it mean I'm going to get a letter inviting me to Hogwarts?" There was an edge of hysteria in my voice.

Less than two hours earlier I'd thought I was a regular girl. Before now, the difficulties of being a closeted lesbian and getting my own car were my biggest worries. Now I was a witch and some evil thing in my basement wanted to kill me.

"All it means is you can do some things most people can't," Lydia, instead of my mom, answered. "Everyone has a touch of the powers, but very few people can actually use them. Of those few, really only a tiny fraction can control them."

"Our family has been living in this area and protecting the crack for centuries," Mom continued.

"Protecting the what?" I asked. I was pretty sure I knew what she meant, but I was still reeling from everything that'd happened.

"Beneath our house is a split between the worlds, a spot where it's very easy to cross back and forth," she said, looking at me quizzically. Then she continued, "I'm not sure who the first of our ancestors were that decided to take up the post of guarding the crack, but I know it happened after the local native population was killed off or driven from the area."

Lydia interrupted the narrative.

"I've done a lot of research on the area. My mom and your gran had a lot of information to sift through amongst themselves and I've been going over all of it since high school." She smiled at me and pushed forward, "The legends of the crack go back as far as humans have inhabited the area. During the French and Indian War, the last of the native guardians were killed and the darkness from the other side began to infest our world."

"I believe that is when our earliest ancestors moved here from Ireland and took up the post. I don't know any of the details, but the way your Gran always told it seemed to indicate we were called here." Mom sighed and rubbed the back of her neck.

"Called by who?" I whispered.

"There's no way to know," Lydia offered. "The God and Goddess, the universe, the last of the native shaman… there's no way to tell, but when your ancestors arrived they managed to push the darkness back into the crack."

"The house was built right on top of it and our family has lived there ever since," Mom finished.

"Why did you bring me here?" I finally asked, finding my voice. "That thing tried to take me when I was little. For that matter, why the hell did you ever let me visit in the first place?!" I was confused and getting angry.

"Ally, distance doesn't mean anything," Mom said quietly. "You could live in China and you would be just as susceptible to that thing as you are now."

Lydia snaked an arm around my shoulder and drew me in tight.

"I left town because I wanted nothing to do with any of this," Mom continued sadly. "I thought if I left I could avoid my mother's life of secret service. I thought the other's in the Coven, like Lydia's mom, would be able to keep the thing in the crack quiet. Then you were born and I knew I'd never get away."

"What do you mean?" I asked, shocked by the shame I heard in my powerful mother's voice. She'd always been the strongest person in the world to me, and now she sounded so small.

"When I saw your light, the power and beauty you radiated, I knew we'd be back here. In all my years, I'd never known a person with a fraction of your power." She looked me in the eyes and now I saw her strength once more. "We brought you here as a girl to see if you would react to the thing. Gran and I thought you might be strong enough to close the crack once more."

"But I'm not and it almost killed me," I mumbled, unexpected heat rushing to my cheeks. There was no reason for me to feel ashamed about not being strong enough, but I was. "I'm sorry."

Mom broke out in loud uncomfortable laughter.

"Sweetie, you have nothing to be sorry about," she snorted.

I looked at her, confused by her words and surprised by her unusual reaction.

Calming down, she then made the pronouncement that would change everything. "Ally, the reason it tried to take you was because it was scared. You're the first being it's ever encountered more powerful than it is."

My mouth dropped open in shock.

Chapter 10

"Confrontation"

I don't know what I expected when we returned to the house.

After the revelations of the evening, I think I'd convinced myself there would be a monster waiting on the doorstep or that looking at the house would produce the same throbbing pain as a rotted tooth lodged in my gums. But when we drove up the long winding driveway and arrived on the property our family had owned for generations I saw... our house.

I could feel the presence of the crack beneath it now. Maybe I've always been able to feel it, but this was the first time I was actively aware of it. As each hour passed, I could feel my abilities, my gifts I guess, increasing in strength. The sight of my home held me fixated as the car cruised to a stop between the house and the barn.

Maybe I should have been afraid of it. I mean, I knew what lived underneath the foundation but I couldn't be. This was the house my mom grew up in. This was the house I spent summers in with Gran and Grandpa Roy. Except for that day when I was little and earlier today when my memories of that day started coming back, I'd never been scared here. Even though I wasn't afraid, I felt like I should be.

And that pissed me off.

This was my home and I was going to be damned if I would let something, make me feel less than safe here. I didn't wait for Mom, when the car came to a halt I unbuckled my belt, threw the door open, and marched towards the back of the house. The image of the basement bulkhead doors burned in my mind.

"Ally, what are you doing?" Mom asked, bolting from the car and racing to catch up with me. "Ally, wait! I don't think this is a good idea."

I wasn't ignoring her but I was so fixated on my goal, I wasn't consciously aware of her words. I rounded the corner of the house and the doors leading under the house came into my line of sight. Never breaking stride, I cleared the distance between me and the low set entrance.

"Please, Ally," Mom said, putting a hand on my shoulder and trying in vain to slow me down. "Ally, can't you hear the music?!"

Her words were enough to bring me somewhat back to reality and I did hear the music. Below what I could actually hear with my ears, the sounds of crickets and cars far in the distance chief amongst them, I heard something else.

It sounded like sickly chamber music. There was a rancid quality to it I could feel in the marrow of my bones. Watery-cold filled my stomach and the moisture left my mouth and eyes. Dry stinging pain filled my ears, eyes, nose, and throat. I slowed, but didn't stop my progress. When I reached the bulkhead I reached down and grasped the handle.

"Ally!" Mom gasped. "Alison, if you open those doors, I'm not going to be strong enough to follow you down there."

Without hesitation, I turned the handle and opened the doors.

From behind me, Mom made a retching sound and released my shoulder. The pungent smell of hot vomit filled the air around me. I could hear her gasping and crying.

"Ally... you're not ready for this," she gasped between gagging spasms. "If you go down there, it could kill you!"

I stopped.

Behind me, Mom was desperately projecting her terror at me. I was still new to these abilities, but I could have felt her fear even if my mind had remained closed. Below me, the darkness beckoned and the intensity of the music increased.

I knew the thing between the worlds, the thing inside the crack, was also afraid. But it also wanted me to enter the basement. It wanted to confront me now and do battle before I knew how to handle my long dormant abilities. I felt a little like Luke Skywalker when Yoda begged him not to leave Dagobah to fight Vader before he was ready.

I paused over the threshold, not backing up and not moving forward. I wanted to go down there and attack. Rage boiled in my belly and I felt like a pressure cooker ready to explode. I rocked back and forth, breathing hard through my nose like a horse ready to break free and run.

Then I heard the voice. It was a dark echoing thing and its power made the fillings in my teeth hurt. Tears streamed from my eyes and a disgusting mixture of snot and blood poured from my nose. My breathing became quick and ragged.

"Come down and face me, child. Come down and let us end this. If you face me I will allow your mother to live... if you don't, I'll feed on her soul and shred her carcass!"

Mom loosened a sickly whimper of pain.

Clarity filled me for the first time since we'd arrived home and I realized what I was about to do, what my rage had spurred me to almost do. I let go of the handle and the door of the bulkhead slammed shut. My breathing became less ragged.

"Not today, you bastard," I growled, looking at the closed doors. "Not today, but soon you're going to have to deal with me."

The sounds of dark music eased and the darkness in my mind cleared. I turned and knelt to help Mom to her feet. She looked pale and sick.

"I'm sorry, Mom," I whispered.

"Don't be sorry," she gasped. "It tried to trick you into fighting and you resisted. I'm so proud of you."

I led Mom into the house, our house, while beneath us the thing raged.

Chapter 11
"Dream Walk - Part 1"

You would have thought sleep was an impossibility considering the day I'd had and the roof I was lying under. But less than a minute after my head hit the pillow, I was sound asleep and snoring loud enough to wake a longshoreman. Apparently I was more exhausted than terrified. I was falling through a familiar and much beloved tunnel between the conscious and unconscious worlds.

I knew I was dreaming.

I've always been a vivid dreamer. Dreams so intense I'd wake gasping in fear, laughing in amusement, or shivering with pleasure, have been a staple in my life. As far back as I can remember, unlike other kids, I loved going to bed. I knew once I was down for the count a new world of adventure would be opened to me. It's like having a second life.

I once told a teacher in seventh grade that I remembered almost all of my dreams and that I could control them. I didn't have the term "Lucid Dreaming" in my repertoire then. She told me that was not possible. According to her, people remembered maybe five percent of their dreams and controlling them was impossible. When I argued, perhaps and bit too passionately, she sent me to the guidance councilor.

That was the last time I talked about my dreams.

So like I've already said, I knew I was dreaming... but this one was different.

I was standing on a hill. The grass beneath my bare feet was green, soft, and warm. All around, trees spread as far as the eye could see. Above, the sun shone brightly in a piercing blue sky. The air smelled of fresh pine and the slight muddy, but comforting, aroma of a distant river. I felt as if I should know where I was.

"Hello, Ally," a female voice said from behind.

In the real world, a strange voice in such tranquility would have startled me. But here in this place, I think I knew all along I was not alone. When I turned to see who was talking to me I wasn't even surprised.

"Hello, Gran,," I said, smiling.

The woman before me was my age and achingly beautiful, but I recognized her from the thousands of picture Mom lovingly cared for in dozens of albums. Short, golden hair framed a pixie face with deep set blue eyes. She was dressed in a simple sun dress and, like me, was barefoot.

She grinned back at me and spread her arms wide.

I rushed into them and, regardless of the form, I knew that embrace. My grandmother's arms would never be anything but a place of comfort and joy, all fear banished within their confines.

"I've missed you, Ally," she said, kissing me on the top of my head.

"I missed you too," I responded, hugging her tighter. Then, reluctantly I released the embrace and pushed forward. "I'm dreaming."

Grandma nodded.

"But this is real, isn't it? This is really you and I'm really here," I finished, spreading my hands to indicate the landscape. "Something has fundamentally changed in me, hasn't it?"

"Yes," Gran said, taking one of my hands in hers. She was warm, almost hot, to the touch. "There's a lot to talk about, and everyone is waiting for you."

"Who's waiting?" I asked, allowing her to lead me down the far slope of the hill and into the dense woods.

"You'll see," Gran replied mysteriously.

I wanted to press her but I had other questions. "Gran, why do I feel like I should recognize this place?"

The young woman with the ancient soul laughed at the question. "Ally, are you telling me you really don't recognize this place?"

I stopped and looked around. She was right, I really should have known where I was, but it was wrong somehow. Thoughts raced through my mind.

There are too many trees.

Where's the river?

The hills are too high.

The valley is hidden in growth.

When it finally hit me, it was like a bolt of lightning through my body. Releasing Grandma's hand, I turned all about and gape in shocked wonder. "I'm home," I whispered.

"Not exactly," Grandma laughed. "This won't be home for either of us for about ten thousand years, give or take a thousand."

"We're in the past?" I asked, shocked by the possibility.

"Sort of... time has no meaning here," she replied, taking my hand again and leading me into the dark coolness of the woods. "We're in the dream stream, Ally. Do you know what that is?"

I shook my head no, but said nothing.

"You entered the psychic plane earlier today when you were breaking through the blockage remembering your past," she said, pushing a branch to the side. "The dream stream is like that but so much more. Everyone touches the dream stream when they sleep. Normal people simply skim the surface and are oblivious to what it is. People like you, me, and the other Guardians... we get the full experience."

"The other what?" I asked, confused and feeling more off balance than when I met Lydia. "Gran, what are you talking about?"

Instead of answering me, she led me through a copes of trees and into a clearing, one I would have recognized even if I was rendered deaf, dumb, and blind. The house and barns were gone and the river was nowhere to be seen, but the place where my home stood in the real world sang to me. The place where the house would stand eons into the future here had a ring of standing trees arranged in a pattern that resembled Stonehenge. I knew that was no coincidence. A small blue and green fire burned in the middle of the ring of trees and a group of women, maybe a hundred, milled within the open space.

"Gran." I hesitated at the perimeter of the circle. "Who are all of those women?" Something in my gut told me to stop. Could I somehow know that if I breached the perimeter of foliage, my life would be changed forever? Maybe, but it's much more likely that I'm a suspicious girl by nature, even in the dream world.

"You know who they are, sweetie," Gran said, squeezing my hand.

And I did—they were the Guardians of the portal. They were the woman charged throughout time with protecting our world from the dangers of the other worlds. Each of them was part of my lineage, either through biology or duty. The power and wisdom of the assemblage was amazing and more than a little intimidating. They were all looking at me.

There was no more hesitation, I stepped into the ring of trees and accepted my destiny.

Chapter 12

"Dream Walk - Part 2"

I couldn't count the number of women within the circle of trees. It wasn't because there were too many, although there were a lot. It was because they kept disappearing and reappearing. Many of the women were more like ghosts, translucent and wispy, rather than solid. They were of all ages, races, and builds. But they all had one thing in common—the same brilliant aura that I also possessed.

"I don't want to be here," I whispered, the ramifications of this moment catching up to me.

"You're free to leave," Gran said, taking my hand and giving it a firm yet tender squeeze. "But you won't, will you, Ally?"

"Why do you say that?" I asked, even as I was unconsciously shaking my head no.

"You know what's at stake. Unlike most of us, you've confronted the thing that dwells below," she said sadly. "You've seen it and walked away with your mind and soul intact."

"I don't want to think about it," I whispered, my voice not that of the adult me, but the one of the little girl who'd gone into the basement.

"I know, sweetie," Gran said. "But the time to turn back has passed as you already sense."

I nodded, fat tears streaming down my face.

"I'm scared," I choked helplessly.

Instead of speaking, she took me into her arms and hugged me tight. I don't know if it was some power of Gran's hug or just because she was my grandmother and I loved her, but my fear dissipated. It didn't completely vanish, but the extreme terror threatening to overwhelm me receded into the background. I was still scared, but the desire to run was gone.

"Better?" Gran asked, releasing and taking my hand once more in hers.

"Yes," I said smiling shyly. "I'm sorry about that."

"Never apologize because you're scared," Gran said, a very familiar sternness in her voice. It was the same voice she used to chastise me with if I took a cookie from the jar without asking permission. "When push comes to shove, Ally, your fear is what will keep you alive. The important thing to remember is you have to control it, not the other way around."

I nodded but my attention drew towards a woman approaching us from the circle. She was small. I doubt if she even scraped five feet tall. Her delicate Native American features and dark indigo eyes were breathtaking. Even in these bizarre circumstances the more prurient part of me wondered what she would look like in silk. Her aura was amazing, a supernova of colors.

"Hello, Alison," she said once she reached us. Her voice had a musical quality to it. "I am pleased to meet you. My name is Quiet Water. I am the first Guardian of the Door."

"Hello," I said, my mind feeling thick and awkward in her presence.

Quiet Water turned to Gran. "Is she ready, Janet?"

"She was born ready," Gran responded. I could feel the waves of pride cascading off her and it filled me with love. "We've always known she would be the one."

Quiet Water nodded.

"What does that mean?" I asked, feeling decidedly confused. "What have you always known?"

From the earliest of my memories I hated to feel as if things were being kept from me. When I was five and my cat Cindy was hit by a truck, my mother tried to keep it from me and tell me she'd run away. I hadn't known how but I knew Mom was lying. Now I understand it was my powers, but even back then I demanded the truth. She told me and I cried for a full day, but in the end the truth is always better.

Anger was building in me and I knew the women could see it in my aura. I could feel the shift from white to crimson all around me, even though I couldn't see it. Power coursed through me, racing from the center of my body to the tips of my toes and fingers. It felt amazing.

"Ally," Gran said, moving back a few steps but never releasing my hand. There was a look of pain on her face. "You need to calm down. You don't understand your power yet. In this place you might be the strongest one, and your anger is amplifying it exponentially."

I almost exploded with irritation. Then I looked at the face of Quiet Water and the other women, all of whom were staring at me. There was real fear in their eyes. With considerable effort, I forced myself to calm. With an effort of will, I shoved the power back into that spot in the center of myself where it lived. I knew I wouldn't be able to keep it locked away for long... nor did I want to.

"I'm sorry," I muttered.

"No," Gran said sadly. "I'm sorry. I tried to protect you from all of this. I let your mother take you away from the farm and I hoped this burden would pass you by. I was wrong. I should have been getting you ready all of your life."

"It is no one's fault," Quiet Water said. "Janet, you wanted your granddaughter to have a normal life. There is no shame in that. It is just chance that she is the one who stands before the door at this time of trial."

The beautiful copper skinned woman looked at me and her face split in an angelic smile. My knees went a little wobbly. Then she reached out and took my other hand in hers. Her power mingled with mine. It wasn't the safety Gran gave me or the love and passion I felt when I touched Lydia—this was sensation of power and age.

"Alison, there are many things you need to know," Quiet Water said.

Gran and Quiet Water led me into the middle of the circle. All around me I saw the women, all of the other Guardians of the Door, looking upon me with expectation. There was palpable fear in the circle. It wasn't overpowering like the fear I'd felt before entering the ring of trees, but it was still strong.

"Sisters," Quiet Water said to the women, "this is Alison."

There was no verbal response but a tidal wave of love and strength spread from them and cascaded over me. The rush was like nothing I'd ever experienced.

"I am the first Guardian," Quiet Water said, raising our hands up high, "and one way or another Alison is the last."

Chapter 13

"Dream Walk Part 3"

I should have been scared. Gran and Quiet Water held my hands in the middle of the circle with a blue and green fire burning coolly between us. The other Guardians, I was never able to get a firm count on them, sat holding hands around the circle's inner perimeter, facing away from us. I should have been terrified, but I wasn't.

"They will face the dangers and shield us from the gaze of the enemy," Quiet Water said when I looked at the other Guardians. "They will cloak us and allow you to walk through the layers of time without worry."

"I still don't understand most of this," I replied.

Gran squeezed my hand and I was filled with a wave of strength and love.

"In order to understand what needs to be done, you must first see what has come before," Quiet Water said, her sing song voice reassuring in its own wonderful way. "Are you ready, Alison?"

I nodded.

"Close your eyes," Gran said.

I never thought to hesitate. I shut my eyes and the same sensation of falling I experienced with Lydia returned, the feeling of my hands being held by Gran and Quiet Water ceased and I was all alone, falling through the void. The fear returned and I acted without thinking.

Lydia! I screamed in my mind. It was just a reflex, and it never occurred to me that my words would have the power they did. *Lydia, please help me!*

My hands were once more being held.

The Void

"Ally, where are we?" Lydia asked, her hands trembling in my own.

I opened my eyes and saw her. She was radiant. I don't know if my powers had grown strong enough to see auras other than my mother's, or if it was a function of where we were, but she was gorgeous. Green and silver lights jumped and swirled like liquid all around her.

"I'm so sorry, Lydia," I said, pulling her into a tight hug. She felt warm and smelled of almonds and vanilla. "I'm supposed to do this alone. I didn't mean to pull you in. I'm so sorry I got scared and—"

Lydia stopped me with a kiss.

"Better, love?" she asked, breaking the kiss and brushing a lock of hair from my face.

"Yes," I said grinning.

"Good, and don't be sorry. If you need me, I'm here no matter what," she replied, looking around the dark emptiness surrounding us. "Umm... Ally, where are we?"

"The beginning," I said.

"The beginning of what?" Lydia asked, giving me crooked smile.

"I think of everything," I replied in a hushed whisper.

Before Lydia could respond, the void all around us exploded in light and heat. It was beautiful and terrifying in equal measure. There was more happening than any human mind, even one as gifted as mine or Lydia's could take in. I think my mind filtered what we were seeing and reinterpreted it as something we could process. Time, space, and reality swirled in a ball of chaos.

"So," Lydia asked, awestruck by racing columns of color and energy, "this is what 'let there be light' means."

I didn't even fight the laugh.

Time moved fast and we watched trillions of galaxies rise and fall. We saw the births and deaths of entire species and civilizations. We were swept toward a small spiral galaxy in an unimportant branch of an inconspicuous globular cluster. The view zoomed in on a section of one arm.

"I think I'm gonna be sick," I muttered.

Lydia slipped an arm around my waist and held me close.

Around a yellow star, a ball of gas and rubble coalesced into a volcanic sphere. A smaller sphere struck it and sheared off a section of the globe, which formed its own small orbiting sphere. The planet cooled and rain fell—the infant primordial Earth stood revealed.

"This is so cool," Lydia whispered.

Over tens of hundreds of millions of years' proteins, then multi-cellular life, then plants, then insects, and then fish erupted across the globe. That was when something unexpected happened, first one, then many holes opened in space, disgorging objects and creatures of indescribable beauty and horror. We saw it in minutes, but in real time it spread over a billion years.

"What are they?" I asked.

"I think they're gods," Lydia said. "We're seeing the arrivals of the Great Old Ones and the Elder Beings."

"The arrival of the what?" I asked, confused and getting scared again.

"I'll explain later," Lydia answered. "I think we're getting close to what you're supposed to see."

The world below us spun. The land moved and the life evolved. Small life led to medium life, led to gargantuan dinosaurs thundering across the globe. Amongst them, the Ancient Beings engaged in their own shenanigans. The rock fell from the sky, directed by fate and chance. The Earth heaved, the animals all but disappeared, and the Ancient Ones retreated beneath the land and waves.

"Oh wow," Lydia whispered.

"You got that right, love," I added, transfixed by the sight below us.

Life started again, small mammals and birds spread from isolated pockets across the devastated globe. The Ancient Ones stayed secreted away as more of their star-spawned brethren arrived. On an island in the Pacific, a race of monstrous creatures and their Elder God King held sway for a millennium before retreating beneath the waves to sleep the sleep of the dead. On an Antarctica devoid of ice, the Elder Things shaped life until their own creations eventually destroyed them, leaving only smashed and frozen ruins. In Africa, primates changed and evolved spreading across the lands of the earth.

"We're almost to the moment," I said, feeling the certainty in my gut.

On a day like any other, less than fifty thousand years ago, it arrived. The dark mass of undulating energy and an indefinable form appeared in orbit and fell to a spot on the North American continent I was intimately familiar with, my home. The creature's impact created the valley our town was nestled in and its form took up residence in the land where our farm now sits.

"That's it," I said, resisting the nearly irresistible urge to pull away and flee. "That's the thing behind the door in my basement."

Time flowed and people moved into the valley. They were quickly put under the thrall of the creature. They were compelled to build temples to it and offer sacrifices in its name. A name I finally learned, Ast-Murath. Ten thousand years ago, he met his end. A young woman amongst the tribe of the valley was born with the power to resist and confront the monster.

"Who is that?" Lydia asked not actually expecting an answer.

"Her name is Quiet Water," I answered. "She was the first Guardian of the Door. She trapped him on the other side of the barrier."

The Circle

One second I was watching Quiet Water banish Ast-Murath to the prison dimension, the next I was sitting in the circle. Now instead of three of us holding hands around the green and blue flame, there were four.

"Hello, Lydia," Gran said, smiling at my love. "What are you doing here, sweetheart?"

"Ally needed me so I came," she answered.

Gran nodded and said no more to her. Turning to me she continued, "Did you see it? Did you see the arrival?"

"Yes," I answered. "I saw the arrival. I saw the banishment and I saw the true history." I turned my gaze to Quiet Water. "Now tell me how to send it away forever."

Chapter 14

"The Next Morning"

I woke up covered in sweat, with Lydia's name on my lips. I've always been a vivid dreamer, but never in my entire life had I experienced anything like that. I remembered every second until I asked Quiet Water what to do and she touched my forehead.

Then all was colors, sounds, and smells.

"What did you do to me?" I muttered, sitting up and clutching my trembling arms under my breasts. Despite having slept, I felt like I'd just finished a marathon. All I wanted to do was go back to bed and log another twelve hours of shut eye.

That being said, I knew I couldn't.

Sliding my legs out from under the quilt Gran made before I was born, I dropped my feet to the floor and moaned. Every muscle ached and the shower stall in my small adjoining bathroom called to me. Boxes, most still sealed from the move, were stacked haphazardly around the room and it took several minutes to locate the things I needed.

"The water better be hot," I muttered, staggering into the lilac painted washroom like an extra in a zombie movie.

It was.

Half an hour and I assume a hundred gallons of hot water later, I was freshly scrubbed and wrapped in my fluffy Jem and the Holograms bathrobe. The smells of fresh coffee were a siren's song and led me down two flights of stairs to the expansive kitchen and dining room that occupied most of the house's first floor. Mom sat at the broad mahogany table, sipping coffee and reading the paper.

"I was wondering if you passed out in the shower. I was just about to come up and check," she said, glancing over the top of the paper and smiling crookedly.

"Long night," I grunted, snatching up a clean mug from the counter and filling it with coffee. I didn't even savor the aroma and instead took a long drink of the very warm strong brew.

"What happened?" Mom asked, closing the paper and going serious.

I held up a finger and polished off the cup before speaking.

"I talked to Gran last night," I finally answered, setting the mug back down and not looking Mom in the eyes. I didn't think I would be able to stand it if the news made her face fall or, goddess forbid, she started crying.

She didn't, but instead asked me another question.

"How is she?" Mom asked softly.

"She's happy," I said, looking up and smiling shyly.

"Good," Mom replied, nodding before taking a drink of her own coffee. Then she continued once more in the serious mom voice she'd always reserved for report cards and parent teacher conferences. "What did she tell you? Was it something that'll help in the current situation?"

"Yes and no," I answered, moving from the counter to take a seat next to her. Mom took one of my hands in both of hers and I continued, "She introduced me to someone who had a lot of the answers I needed."

For the next hour I gave Mom a complete rundown of everything that'd happened. When I got to the part where Quiet Water touched my forehead, I did my best to convey the information, which was really just random impressions, but in the end I petered out and shrugged my shoulders in frustration.

"It's all right, Ally," Mom said, getting up and wrapping her arms around me.

In that instant, I was a little girl again, and she was my mommy trying to explain why my daddy wouldn't be coming home, without telling me he didn't want to have anything to do with me. I buried my face in her chest and wept openly, with no shame. I could feel her emotions and there was nothing but love and pride radiating from her. It was shocking how quickly I was getting used to this and I wondered why that was. As if on cue, Mom answered in my mind.

You could always feel my thoughts and emotions, but only in the background not in the front of your mind. So many times, when you were awake, I wanted to speak like this with you but I was afraid doing that would open your mind to the thing behind the door. I know, foolish but the truth, she said, rocking back and forth stroking my still damp hair.

When I was awake? I asked, feeling there was more to this.

I couldn't help myself. When you were little and sleeping I'd—

You'd sing to me in my sleep! I exclaimed looking up at her. *I thought those were dreams!*

Mom laughed in my mind and hugged me tighter. For several minutes I allowed myself to take in all the comfort and maternal warmth she had to offer. Our emotions danced together and for the first time in my life all of the teenager/parent crap was gone. She was my mother and I was her daughter. She was also my best friend and I knew the only way I'd make it through this was with her at my side.

"I'll be with you until the end," she said out loud. "But I'm not sure how much help I'll be. Compared to the power you have, I'm a spark in the darkness."

"Not to me you're not," I said fiercely.

Mom kissed my forehead and disengaged from me reluctantly. "What do we do next?" she asked, taking her seat once more.

"It's all a confused jumble," I admitted. "But there are a few things we'll need before I even consider going back into the basement, let alone opening that door."

Mom nodded but said nothing.

"After breakfast I need to talk to Lydia," I finished.

"That's a good idea," Mom said. "I'm out of touch with the old community. She'll know who we need to talk with to get what you need."

"What old community?" I asked, confused.

"Sweetie," Mom said as a genuine, broad smile filled her face and transformed her from a lovely middle aged woman to a stunning young lady. "You didn't think we were going to have to do this all on our own, did you?"

Chapter 15

"The Next Morning"

I'd expected to head back to Moon Dust after breakfast, but Mom told me they were coming to us. The change in the dynamic between me and Mom was so overwhelming I was almost able to forget there was a monster determined to see me dead right under my feet. It was kinda insane to be feeling this good. I knew this was going to be the last normal day we'd have. We were living in the eye of the proverbial storm, and I was determined to enjoy it and remember it when things weren't so good.

They arrived an hour after my shower.

There were seven of them not including Lydia, five women and two men. I didn't like the way they looked at me when they entered our home. There was a look of reverence in their eyes that made me very uncomfortable. They were all mingling in the family room, most of them greeting my mother with hugs and kisses on the cheek, but they all kept stealing sidelong glances at me.

I guess it was becoming obvious that I was getting agitated because suddenly there was a warm familiar hand grasping my own.

Calm down, love, it's okay, Lydia said in my mind. *These are my friends. These are the people your mom and mine grew up with. This is the Moon Dust Coven and they're here to help.*

I squeezed and felt the anxiety wash away.

When your mom called them, they all kinda freaked out and ended up at the shop. They're scared, but they know what needs to be done, Lydia continued. *I know it's not fair but you have to do your best to calm them down, sweetie.*

You know I'm scared too, I replied, putting a false smile on my face.

I know, but you've faced the thing and come away with your body and soul intact. These people are all positive they're going to die today and I'm not sure they're wrong, Ally, Lydia finished. I felt her fear and sadness like a cloak wrapped around her body.

The decision to act firmed instantly.

"Hey!" I said in a tone just below a yell.

Everyone gathered in the living room stopped talking and fixed their eyes on me.

The focus of so many people projecting their fears and desire for reassurance on me was nearly crippling. I was still getting used to the mercurial nature of the human spirit. Each of them shone with their own vibrant light, and I fought the reflex to shield my eyes from the glow. These people were here of their own free will, and they needed me to set the tone.

"I'm really glad you're all here, and I know my mom is happy to see all of you again," I said. "As much as I wish you could all catch up, I think we need to talk about what's about to happen."

The group of people, all radiating fear and unease, remained stone silent.

Lydia gripped my hand tighter, if that was possible.

One woman, clearly the oldest and the leader of the group, stepped forward. The vibe coming off her was more anger than fear. This one was not happy to see me, and the red shift in her aura was all the confirmation that we weren't allies that I needed.

That's my Aunt Ellen, Lydia thought at me. *She's not happy about any of this.*

That makes two of us, love, I responded.

"What we need to talk about is why you prodded that thing under this house," she said, lips pursed.

"Ellen, that's not what happened," Mom said, moving from the group and approaching me. "As soon as we arrived, it reached out and touched her again."

"Everything was fine here until you returned, Rebecca," Ellen snapped.

"That's not true, Aunt Ellen," Lydia said.

I felt the fire burning in her. The righteous indignation on my behalf was intense and I have to admit kind of intoxicating. My toes tingled and I had to fight the urge to kiss Lydia until neither of us could breathe.

"Quiet, Lydia," the woman snapped, never breaking eye contact with Mom.

"If you think things were fine then you're a bigger fool now than you were when I left," Mom snapped.

I could feel her rolling up her mental sleeves and I was reminded of the rare occasions when I was little and she was forced to punish me… that time I colored in her first edition of *The Old Man and the Sea* being the most prominent on my memories. Now that I could see her inner light, it was even more terrifying.

"You ran away, Becky," Ellen growled. "You left the coven, hell you left the entire state, and you no longer have any say in this."

"This is my home," Mom snapped, advancing on the taller woman. "Ally is my daughter," she continued, coming nose to nose with her. "You will *not* dictate to me, Ellen!"

"Back off, Becky," Ellen whispered so softly she was almost silent. "Back off right now or you'll be sorry."

As the two women squared off, the others in the room were physically and mentally retreating to the far side of the room, leaving Mom, Ellen, Lydia, and myself in the center of an emotional maelstrom.

Stop! I screamed with my mind.

All I was trying to do was stop the fight before it started. I didn't want to hurt anyone. Unfortunately I had no idea how powerful I was. Lydia was the only one spared and that was because we were already connected and she knew what was coming a fraction of a second before it happened. It was just enough time for her to pull up a mental defense.

Every man and woman in the room, except for Lydia and me, collapsed to the floor, clutching their heads. You'd have thought howls of pain would've filled the room, but instead there was only the collective muted whimper of agony.

I wanted to run to Mom and help her up, but this needed to end now. Setting my mental feet, I opened my mind wide to these people and spoke.

If you're not here to help then get the hell out. The past doesn't matter anymore. Ast-Murath is awake and he's going to attempt his escape. Either we stand together and fight him or we run, hide, and eventually die alone and afraid in the dark.

Ellen raised her head, blood trickling from her nose, and looked at me. I think she was actually seeing me for the first time and taking my measure. Slowly she nodded her agreement.

Stepping forward, I offered her my hand and she took it.

"Good," I said out loud. "We have a lot to do and very little time to do it."

Chapter 16

"Standing Up"

"Did I hurt you?" I asked my mom. I was terrified that in my anger and frustration I might have hurt her.

"No," she whispered. She was still sitting on the floor, holding a hand to her head and drawing her knees to her chest. "But I wasn't ready for a sonic boom in my skull. I doubt anyone but Lydia was."

At the sound of her name, I turned my head to see my girl helping others to their feet and doing her best to calm them. Pride and love flashed through my body. Of course she'd been prepared, she was the other half of my heart. I think she could feel my mind turn towards her because she turned her head to me and smiled.

"That happened fast," Mom said.

"What?" I asked, turning back to her, confused.

"You and Lydia," she laughed. "How long were you with her before I called you, an hour and a half?"

"Maybe," I replied, blushing and feeling a little too exposed.

"As long as you're happy," Mom said, indicating she was ready to stand up.

I stood, took her proffered hand, and helped her come shakily to her feet. She was the first person affected to get back up. Her strength through all of this was inspiring. If I had her and Lydia at my side I might just be able to survive this.

"I think, Becky," Ellen said, struggling to her own feet, "now that we know where everyone stands we need to discuss the situation." Reluctantly she turned and looked at me before continuing, "I have a bad feeling our time is short."

I nodded, not trusting myself yet to not tear into her.

"Agreed," Mom replied, also looking at me. "This is your show now, Ally. What do we do now?"

I looked at the group of middle aged men and women. They were all making me uncomfortable. Their collective gaze seemed to be begging me to save them, to give them a wall to lean against so they didn't have to feel alone, naked, and exposed to the coming darkness. A tight ball of cold fear exploded in my gut and the urge to run became damn near irresistible. Then Lydia was there, in my mind, holding me in her embrace.

I knew when she was near I'd never have to be afraid again.

"I think..." I started, my voice cracking.

And with that the tension was broken. First Mom, then Lydia, and then one by one every member of the coven broken into a fit of giggling until at last even me and Ellen were laughing. Maybe it was genuine and maybe it was just me projecting my habit of laughing when I was nervous, but regardless it did the trick. While not banished, the fear, tension, and anger were pushed far into the background to be replaced by a sense of unity and fellowship I'd never experienced before.

It was intoxicating.

"It's a beautiful day," I said once the laughter was reduced to isolated chuckles. "Why don't we move this entire thing out to the picnic table under the apple tree?"

"I think that's a wonderful idea," Mom said, gesturing to the porch door.

One by one they flowed, some steadier than others, out of the living room with Mom in the lead, chatting and laughing. It was a complete one hundred and eighty degree switch from when they arrived. Then only Lydia, Ellen, and me were remaining in the house and it was clear there was still business to be attended to.

"Lydia," Ellen said, never taking her eyes off of me, "maybe you should go outside with the others."

"That's all right, Lyd, you're fine just where you are," I said coolly.

"No, it's okay," Lydia replied, wrapping her arms around me and hugging me tight. "I think I'd rather be out under the sun. Besides you've got this," she added, giving me a very-not-just-friends kiss.

I wouldn't have believed what happened next if I hadn't seen it. My girl walked right up to Ellen, a woman radiating power and old enough to be her mom, leaned in close and hissed at her with a smile plastered on her beautiful elfin face.

"If you do or say anything to upset her, I will make you sorry, you old hag."

Ellen looked as if she'd been punched in stomach. She said nothing as Lydia left to join the others outside. Just as she stepped out, Lydia turned her head and winked at me, then she was gone and we were alone.

"She does not like you very much," I said when I couldn't take the silence anymore.

"No," Ellen agreed, collecting her composure. "Well it's to be expected. Her mother and I didn't end things on good terms and there wasn't any time to try and fix things after the accident."

"So you weren't exactly anxious to leave with the rest of the group," I said, ignoring all the questions about Lydia and my mom that I wanted to ask Ellen. "What do you want?" There was a hesitation and I swear I could hear an audible mental click before she spoke.

"Can you do this?" she asked bluntly.

"What do you mean, can I do this?" I shot back, surprised at the naked desperation I heard in her voice and saw in her aura. Ellen was terrified.

Can you shut the gods damned door?! she screamed in my head.

"You've seen it," I said out loud. "The others are scared, but not like you. You're scared like I'm scared, like my Gran was scared. You've touched it... you've heard the music."

Ellen went chalk white and her eyes dilated. I knew she was going to pass out. Moving fast, I managed to catch her body a heartbeat before her head hit the edge of the ancient table that dominated the room. I didn't mean to go into her mind but the stress coupled with my hand touching bare skin in her neck was all it took.

One second I was on the floor of the living room and the next I was falling down the rabbit hole... again. But this time there was no Lydia to guide me.

Chapter 17

"Back Down the Rabbit Hole"

I felt like I was falling down a bottomless shaft and this time my love wasn't there with me. I was less unnerved this time than when Lydia and I travelled into the void after we first met. But that's like saying after you've been saved from drowning the sensation is a known quantity... in other words I was still piss scared. My hand, at least the mental representation of my hand, held one of the unconscious Ellen's firmly as we fell.

The silence was deafening.

I knew time had no meaning on this side of the veil, but it felt like hours passed before anything happened. To tell the truth and shame the devil, which was one of Gran's all-time favorite sayings, I was getting really bored when Ellen spoke. We were in her mind so I guess I shouldn't have been surprised that she needed to come around before this party could really get started.

"Where are we?" Ellen mumbled.

In the void. Her whisper was like a gunshot and I squeaked reflexively.

"What?!" Ellen demanded, her voice going sharp as she realized they were no longer in the farmhouse or even on Earth. "What happened, Alison. What did you do?"

"Hate to disappoint you but it wasn't me, Ellen," I snapped, irritation rising up despite my best efforts. I just didn't like her. "You collapsed and when I touched your skin to catch you before you hit your head, you dragged me into the darkness with you."

"Oh," Ellen responded in a smaller, much quieter voice.

Before either of us could say anything next, the music started playing. At first it chimed so low I thought I was imagining it, but the exponential increase in volume washed all doubt away. Once more, the chill, fear, and nausea exploded from the base of my skull and pit of my stomach. Sounds, sights, smells, and emotions tore through me like a supernatural tsunami.

Ellen whimpered and squeezed my hand in terror.

"Hold on, Ellen," I cried out, trying hard not to release the nonexistent contents of my gut across the void. I wasn't Lydia I was holding on to and I didn't know what to do. "This is your mind, Ellen, you have to concentrate and guide us out of here," I pleaded, tears streaming down my cheeks. My heart hammered so hard I was sure we were about to reenact some of the gorier scenes from the Alien movies.

"I can't," Ellen whimpered. "Please, I can't do it. I don't want to see it again."

I wanted to reach out and smack her as hard as I could. On one hand I understood the fear she was feeling better than maybe anyone else currently alive. Part of me felt bad for her, but the larger part of me wanted off this dark and terrible ride, and I had to make her act I'd do it and apologize later. I turned my head to look the older woman in the eyes.

Open your mind, Ellen! I ordered her mentally.

Ellen's eyes went wide with fear and shock. *What are you doing to me?* her mind whispered back. *Get out of my head!*

I'm sorry, Ellen, I thought, and actually for the life of me meant it. Then without further hesitation I forced my way inside.

Images rushed by and snapshots of Ellen's life flitted through my mind. I saw a young girl of maybe five using her new telepathy to tell her kitten she loved him. An Ellen of twelve experiencing her first out of body experience, and three young women standing in a circle under the stars, hands locked. One was Ellen. One looked so much like my Lydia that my breath caught in my chest. And the third was a version of my mother maybe three years older than I was now.

We hit the ground, or whatever you call it on the mental plane, with a solid thump.

"Where are we?" I asked, getting to my knees and doing my best to calm my breathing.

"How the hell should I know?" Ellen coughed, rolling onto her back and lacing her hands across her eyes. "You're the one who brought us here," she added accusingly.

"Oh hell no," I hissed getting to my feet. "This is your rabbit hole, not mine lady."

There was no response from the prone form of Ellen.

"I'm pretty sure I can leave you here if I concentrate hard enough," I muttered, taking in our surroundings. It was far from a shock to see we were on the farm. Everything always leads back to the farm and the door.

"Whatever," Ellen sighed, "maybe I'm better off in here than out there."

"When are we?" I asked. Light snow blanketed the ground, reflecting the bright moonlight from the cloudless sky. It was hauntingly beautiful.

"We're on your farm," Ellen said, getting shakily to her feet and scanning the surroundings.

"I know that, but the shed for the propane generator isn't here so it's before I was five," I said turning to look at her. "This is one of your memories. When did it happen?"

"Long time ago," Ellen answered, sounding deflated. "This was the last Winter Solstice before your mother left the coven."

"The year I was conceived," I whispered, more to myself than to Ellen, but she responded anyway.

"Yeah, the year before," Ellen hissed.

"And that pisses you off why?" I asked.

"Maybe if we survive all of this your mother will tell you a few things she should've been up front about from the beginning," Ellen said, striding past me and making a beeline for the trees in the distance.

I hurried to catch up. Reaching her side and matching her pace, I demanded answers. "How about you give me the IMDB version now, and I'll deal with my mother later."

"You don't want to know," Ellen said.

She clearly knew something, and for a second I wondered if I should just drop it for now. But I am who I am. Mom's said, on more than one occasion, that I should be a lawyer considering how single-minded I can be when I have a mystery to solve. I grabbed Ellen's shoulder and spun her around mid stride.

"What do you know?!"

"I know who your father is, not that poor sweet man who raised you until he died, I mean your real father," she said, cold anger saturating her voice.

"What the hell are you talking about?" I asked, unconsciously withdrawing from her. "Who's my real father?"

"Alison," she said, a dark smile splitting her lips. "Your real father lives behind the door in the basement.

Chapter 18

"Circle"

"I don't believe you," I whispered not wanting to admit her words had the distinctive ring of a very unpleasant truth.

As we stood in the middle of the memory three young women, maybe my age or a touch older, appeared from the ether and headed toward the trees. The very trees I knew contained the ancient circle of the Guardians.

"Why are you whispering?" Ellen asked doing a bad job of ignoring the girls. "This is a memory. I told you it all happened about seventeen years ago. You're almost seventeen right?" she asked and grinned darkly at the pained expression I knew was plastered on my face. "Aren't you a lucky little girl, most people would never even entertain the idea they would one day be able to witness their conception."

I wanted to hit her. The city girl in me wanted to punch the boney, smug bitch right in the chops, but I didn't. Not because I abhor physical violence or because I was afraid of the woman standing next to me, but because my eyes were locked on one of the young women heading into the circle of trees. One I would've recognized anywhere. I ignored Ellen and her acid-filled words and headed toward the circle.

To follow my mother.

It wasn't a circle anymore—trees and shrubs had grown wild over the centuries leaving only a small bare patch where the expansive clearing once held sway. And yet I could still see the old circle of standing trees and defined borders, the place where I learned my destiny and my fate. Like a double exposed image from an old camera or a bad photoshop effect, I saw what was, and what had once been.

"Alison we need to leave," Ellen said joining me in the circle. Her anger and venom having vanished as quickly as they'd come.

"I thought you wanted me to see my father?" I asked darkly. Let's be honest and shame the devil, I didn't like this woman at all.

"I'm sorry I said that," Ellen replied and I knew she meant it. There was a good person buried somewhere in her old anger and regrets. "I can't see this again. Please, it's too much."

"Then leave," I said watching the girls lay out their candles. My mother and a woman I knew was Lydia's mother drew a circle and pentagram in the clearing while another who had to be a very young Helen hung objects from the trees.

"What are you hanging?" I asked.

"Protective totems. We were naïve, but not completely stupid," Helen replied. "And as for me leaving," she continued sounding scared, "we're anchored together, while you're here, I'm here."

"I'm sorry about that," I said and did my best to project the truth of my words to her. "But I think you brought me here because I needed to see this even if you didn't know it."

Helen said nothing.

Candles lit, the three girls joined hands in the middle of the circle.

"Why are the three of you doing this?" I asked turning to look at Helen.

"We wanted to know what the big deal was," she said, her eyes locked on the circle. "None of the elders in the coven would tell us what the purpose was. We didn't understand the depth of the horror we guarded. We didn't understand the magnitude of the responsibility. All we knew was that one of us would be the next Guardian when your grandmother passed on and whoever that was was destined to spend the rest of their life here on this mountain."

"I thought that the mantle passed from mother to daughter?" I asked a little confused.

In the circle, the three girls began chanting and rotating counter clockwise, hands held tight.

"Usually, but when we were all in our preteen years, your grandmother had a vision. In the vision, she saw that it would be one of the three of us who'd be the next guardian, but that the last guardian would be the daughter of your mother." She looked at me and the fear, sadness, and regret I saw made me ill. "She was shown that no matter who the next guardian was, her own granddaughter would be the last."

The air in the center of the circle started glowing a pulsating white and green.

"We needed to know what we were being groomed for," Helen

whispered. "We needed the answers our mothers wouldn't give us."

"It's cold," I said, the breath clear in front of my face. It never dawned on me that I wasn't physically there, and therefore, there was no breath to fog in front of my face. Such was the power or thought and imagination.

"It was winter," Helen replied then continued before I could continue, "but yes, the temperature dropped significantly when we started the ritual. We couldn't feel any of it until we were done though, inside the circle the temperature rose to uncomfortable levels."

"But what—" I started to ask before Helen cut me off.

"Be quiet now and watch!" the woman hissed. "You may be powerful, but you don't know everything, Alison. Pay attention because I think you're right, I think this is important."

I shut up, reached out with my mind and watched... later I wished I hadn't.

Inside The Circle

It was so hot inside the circle, and Becky could feel the sweat erupting all across her body. In front of her, the light pulsated faster than the eye, or the mind could track.

"Becky?" Helen asked questioningly. Her hand gripped Becky's so tight blood flow was cut off and Becky felt her fingers going numb. "Becky what's happening?"

Becky didn't answer her best friend—she was as confused as Helen was.

"This isn't right," Lizzy said from her other side of their triangle. "We should have transitioned to the astral plane, why is there a physical manifestation?"

Music filled the circle, beautiful distant music which nevertheless filled the three young women with dread. The light in the center of the circle changed from white and green to a muddy rainbow of colors. There was nothing pretty or joyful in the hellish carnival lights.

"We have to stop!" Becky said trying to be heard over the increasing sounds of the music.

"Let go and it should break the spell," Lizzy said.

Both girls attempted to break their triumvirate only to find their hands were sealed together in an unbreakable bond. Lizzy and Becky looked at one another with identical faces filled with terror.

"Why?" Helen asked, her voice distant and slurred.

The other girls turned their heads as one to look at their friend. Helen's skin, usually smooth and flush with life looked drawn and pale. Her eyes had gone a milky white, and her hair floated around her head in a dancing halo of brown curls.

"Why would you want to stop when the fun is just starting?" Helen continued, her visage changing before her friend's eyes. Hair shortened, breasts deflated, her musculature changed, and Helen's voice deepened. "Why would you want to leave when you've brought me this wonderful vessel?"

Outside the Circle

"Who is that?" I asked with a dropping sensation, I already knew who it was.

"That Alison," Helen said her head cast down, "is your father."

Chapter 19

"The Decision"

I heard the sounds of laughter from outside, but my eyes remained firmly shut. I couldn't get the images of what'd I'd seen inside of Helen's head out of my mind. They were etched on my brain like the shadows of the dead in Nagasaki and Hiroshima—forever burned into the crumbled walls and shattered buildings. I heard crying I assumed came from Helen and fought the unbearable urge to tell her to shut the hell up.

But I didn't.

"Alison?" a voice asked. At first, I was confused. My head felt like it was filled with the mental equivalent of wet cotton. How can Helen be saying my name when I can still hear her clearly crying over the sounds of the people outside? "Alison, are you okay?"

I opened my mouth to respond when I realized I couldn't. Shocked, I realize I was the one crying. Not only am I crying, but I am wailing hysterically with my arms wrapped across my stomach, gripping my sides and rocking violently back and forth.

Arms wrap around me and drew me in tight.

"Alison," Helen murmured, stroking my back and slowing my rocking. "I'm so sorry you had to see all of that. I swear I didn't take you there on purpose."

"It can't be true," I gasped. "That thing can't be my father." My sobs rendered my words intelligible, but as I spoke, I also projected my thoughts. It was a reflex, and I didn't realize I was doing it until the deed was done.

The conversations and laughing outside ceased.

I kept my eyes shut tight hoping against hope that if I didn't open them and see the world around me, the horrors from the past I'd just witnessed would be negated. I knew I was acting like a child who was certain if she just slept everything would be different in the morning, but considering the mental and emotional trauma I'd endured in Helen's memories maybe I can be forgiven my weakness and desire to deny reality. Despite my physical blindness, my mind saw everything in painful detail.

Mom, followed quickly by Lydia, raced from the picnic table under the apple tree directly toward the house. They'd heard my cries in their mind, and I could feel their concern and terror across every inch of my body. My skin broke out in goosebumps, and a cold sweat covered me like a slimy second skin.

"Alison, please wake up," Helen whispered, drawing me onto her lap and wrapping her arms around me. "Please wake up. I'm sorry," she finished kissing me on the forehead.

"Ally!" Mom yelled bursting into the room and taking in the sight. I could feel the fear in her heart being eclipsed by anger. Rage built within my mother, and I knew she was blaming Helen for what had happened to me. Her rage was quickly overshadowed by Lydia's own, which flared like a blast furnace.

"Mom, Lydia, no," I whispered reluctantly sliding from Helen's maternal embrace and forcing my eyes open. The two most important people in my life stood above me and without meaning too I saw the scene through their eyes. Helen and I were spread out on the floor looking like the dazed survivors of a shipwreck that for some reason were left dry.

Despite my fear and shocked horror at what I'd experienced in Helen's mind, I laughed hard at the insane image. Apparently Lydia saw it all through my eyes as well and joined in—our connection had reestablished without either of us trying. The absurdity of the image, especially in the mundane surroundings of the farmhouse, was too funny not to laugh at. I mean seriously this was a classic laugh or scream moment, and that thing beneath my feet wasn't going to make me scream again.

"What's so funny?" Mom demanded, her anger still in place, but wavering.

"All of this," I said struggling to get to my feet. Once I was up, I offered my hand to Helen, who took it and squeezed hard. The relief in her eyes that I didn't hate her or blame her was so raw and painful it hurt. "We are standing above a portal to hell, where a group of middle-aged witches and their children are trying to figure out how to save the world, but to look at us we all appear to be getting ready for a Sunday farm picnic. This story is so crazy even some hack writer wouldn't have the nerve to publish it."

Mom stared at blankly me for a handful of heartbeats before she broke into fits of her throaty laughter. That laugh, the one I'm sure I can remember from before I was even born, was the most beautiful sound in the world. And just like that my fear and shock melted away to be replaced by love and hope.

I'm not sure who started it but before I knew I was happening the four of us were bound in a communal embrace quickly followed by the merging of minds and hearts. I got it at that moment—I understood why these men and women came together in fellowship despite the dangers from the other worlds. The light and safety of touching on that level were intoxicating. It wasn't the rawness of my bond with Lydia, but in its own way it was just as intense, it was family.

"What happened when you and Helen traveled, Ally?" Mom asked both with her mind and her mouth. I could feel her reluctance to ask. Her desire to enjoy this bit of peace was obvious, but there were serious matters to be dealt with.

"She saw, Becky," Helen whispered. "I'm so sorry. When I collapsed, she entered my mind and she saw the night in the circle. She saw you, me, Lizzy..." Helen hesitated a choke caught in her throat.

"I saw my father," I interrupted sparing Helen the pain of verbalizing and recalling the scene again so soon. "I saw the night I was conceived. I saw what that thing did to you."

Mom withdrew and as soon as it was born our fellowship broke.

Chapter 20

"Pause Button"

Right now I'm standing in the doorway leading from the living room to the outside. Mom and Helen left to check on the rest of the coven, and I asked Lydia to go with them. She wasn't happy about it, and I think when we finally consummate our new relationship I'm going to learn my love can hold a bit of a grudge when her feelings are hurt.

But I needed a few minutes to myself.

I needed to take a moment and breathe.

I know you're anxious to hear how this all ends, but we need to put the breaks on for a second. We've reached the final arc in this story, my story, so humor me and let's take a second and think about all of it.

The day is absolutely gorgeous, the sun high in the bright sky, with the smell of apples and lilacs on the air. Under the big oak tree where the tire swing had hung for decades, more than a dozen people were gathered around the handmade picnic table—the one Grandpa made from the fallen hickory tree when Mom was a girl. The talk, the food, the good vibes all combined to make it feel like a family reunion. Which in many ways it was.

But of course, we all know it wasn't.

First and foremost it was a war council. The entire Moon Dust

Coven was gathered for one purpose above all others. That purpose was to finally seal the barriers and banish the thing living behind the door in the basement. To close off our dimension, our universe, our world from the reach of one of the oldest and darkest beings in existence.

We had to stop Ast-Murath. We had to stop my father.

I know what you're thinking right now, some form of, "Ally, that sounds insane!"

I agree. If I hadn't experienced it in the memories of Helen, one of my mom's oldest friends I wouldn't believe it either. I was raised by my mother, but I remember the man who I knew as Daddy. Sergent 1st Class Christan Poole never came home from the sand and rock of Afghanistan, but he will always be my father no matter what I've learned since.

But none of that changes what is.

One night, more than sixteen years earlier, my mother was raped and impregnated by a being from outside of space and time. The truth is I am not entirely human. The truth is I am the only one who might have a chance at stopping my father from entering our dimension and destroying everything in his wake.

Right now I know some of you are thinking, "Bullshit! This is Raven's story from Teen Titans. Maybe you need antipsychotics or something, Ally."

I am the definition of a comic book geek despite all the menanist assholes saying girls can't like comics. I know this all sounds like something written by Marv Wolfman, but you're just going to have to trust me. This is all real, this all happened.

Everyone has a coward living in them. I believe this as much as I believe in the inevitability of the summer rains. I stood in that doorway, and I'm ashamed to admit for a moment I considered running. I thought about leaving the farm and finding somewhere to hide. I'd leave the two people I loved most in the world to the ministrations of my father and never look back. At that moment I met the coward I could all too easily be, and I was tempted.

That was when I heard him.

Not Ast-Murath, there was none of the sickening music or blinding darkness. No, what I heard was a voice I had not heard since I was little, a voice which had sung me to sleep when I was sick, a voice that read me Harry Potter every night.

I heard the voice of my daddy.

"Hello Ali-Gator," he said so clear in my mind it was like he was standing right by me. The use of my childhood nickname, the one I hadn't let anyone else use after he died, stirred butterflies in my stomach.

"Daddy?" I whispered. I was terrified this was just a hallucination and when I spoke he'd be gone.

"It's me, sweetie," he responded.

"How is that possible?" I asked standing stock still, my eyes unfocused.

"I don't know," he laughed. I would've known that laugh anywhere. "I just knew you needed me, and here I am."

"I'm scared, Daddy," I said. My throat felt swollen and constricted as I spoke.

"I know," he answered.

I felt a hand on my shoulder and I had to fight not to let out a yelp of shock. Slowly I was turned around and found myself staring into the handsome, stubbled face of my real father, the father of my heart. He was more handsome than I remembered.

"It's okay to be afraid Ali-Gator. It's one of the things that makes us human." He smiled, and it lit up the room.

"I might die," I said so quiet I wasn't sure I'd spoke.

"You might," he agreed with a solemn nod. "But Ally, death isn't the end. In some ways, it's really just the beginning."

"What should I do, Daddy?" I asked.

"I can't tell you what to do, Ally. This is your burden, your decision," he said sadly.

I opened my mouth to speak, but he continued.

"I was scared that day in the mountains. I knew I might die, but I had a job to do. Not the one, the politicians talk about, not my responsibilities to flag and country. I had more than a dozen of my buddies with me who counted on me." He smiled at the memory. "I did my job."

"You died, Daddy," I said an unbidden tear rolling down my face.

"Yes I did," he agreed. "But none of my friends did. Every one of them made it home in the end."

He began to fade.

"I miss you, Daddy," I said throwing my arms around him and hugged him for all I was worth.

"We'll be together again Ali-Gator," he responded squeezing back. "And always remember, I'm so proud of you."

Then he was gone and I was alone again.

Outside the Moon Dust Coven socialized and shared fellowship except for Lydia. She stood apart from the rest, her eyes locked on me. She'd seen it all, she understood. I stepped out into the sun and smell of apples. There was work to be done and little time to do it.

Chapter 21
"Standing On The Threshold"

The bulkhead doors leading to the basement stared at me like an accusing face. The grain and patterns of the steel reinforced wooden doors had a haunting Karloff Frankenstein look to them. I could feel a pulsating cold emanating from them despite the warmth of the day and the music, that horrible evil music that would haunt my nightmares for the rest of my life no matter how long or short that might be, was back with a vengeance.

"We could wait," Lydia said, her hand slipping into mine. "We could reach out to some of the other groups we know and get help." There was a sadness mixed in with the fear in her voice. She knew what my answer would be. How couldn't she? She lived in my mind now.

Thankfully I wasn't the one who responded.

"No," Mom said. Her voice was so firm, so confident, that I could feel the assembled Moon Dust Coven unconsciously echo her. "The longer we wait, the stronger it gets and the stronger it gets, the harder this will be."

"Alison coming home woke it up again," Helen added.

Lydia turned to say something harsh to the woman, but the words died unspoken in her mind when she saw Helen's face. The antagonism and anger at my mother was, if not gone, then pushed down so far they might never resurface. All that was there now was fear and truth.

"Maybe it would've been better if Alison stayed away for a few more years," Helen continued, her eyes locked on the doors to the basement. The crows feet at the corners of her gray eyes seemed to deepen as she spoke. "But maybe not."

She turned her gaze toward my mother and in that moment I saw how deeply the old friends still loved one another. "Maybe this is exactly the right moment. The creature was not ready and Alison..." She looked at me and smiled the first warm and genuine smile I'd seen grace her face. At that moment she was seventeen and beautiful once more. "Ally, you're strong, so much stronger than you realize. Maybe right now we have a chance to seal this gateway once and forever."

The group murmured their agreement.

The music continued to increase in intensity, and a sickening, rotting vegetable smell filled my nostrils.

"It's time," I said squeezing Lydia's hand hard.

"Alright people," Mom said, her voice brooking no nonsense. It was a voice I knew too well. It was the voice she used to tell me the laundry better be put away before I went out. It was also the voice she used to assure me everything would be alright when Daddy didn't come home. It was a mother's voice and I loved her more than ever before. "We all know what we need to do. We've always known."

More murmurs mixed with a few nervous laughs.

"We have this, Ally," Helen said. "You just do what you have to do, and we'll do our best to have your back."

I hugged Helen. I had no idea I was going to do it until I was actually wrapping my arms around her. She stiffened in shock and then seemed to gratefully surrender to the embrace. It lasted a moment before we broke the embrace. I'm not sure if her cheeks were damp, but I knew mine were. Helen headed back to the group to get them ready.

I turned to Mom.

"It's always been the Poole women against the world," I said grinning at her and doing my best to ignore the pain on her face. Of course, I failed.

"I'm so—" Mom started, but I cut her off.

"You have nothing to be sorry about," I said. "This is all happening like it's supposed to. I can feel it."

Tears built in her eyes but did not fall.

"Mom," I whispered. "I saw Daddy. I hugged him."

Her hand balled into a fist and went to her mouth in an attempt to stifle a gasp.

"He's happy," I plowed ahead. "He loves us."

Mom choked back a sob and instead of speaking threw her arms around me and spoke into my mind.

I love you, Ally, and I am so proud of you.

I love you, Mommy.

There was nothing more to say, anything else would've been killing time. There was work to be done, terrifying but important work.

I broke the hug and went to the double doors set in the ground.

It's funny what you notice when you're heading to your probable death and the hands of your demon father who's trapped between worlds. I could hear the engine of a small plane in the distance, probably one of the local crop dusters. The river over the hill burbled and if I concentrated, I could feel the flicker of the fish making their way through the icy mountain water. I did my best to ignore the rotten smell and the sound of the music.

"And then there was just thee and me," Lydia whispered.

I nearly jumped at the sound of her voice. Truth be told, I'd forgotten she was there. Or to be more precise I'd forgotten she was a separate person—that was how deeply we'd bonded in the insanely short amount of time we'd known one another.

It felt like a heartbeat... it felt like an eternity.

"I'm scared," I said turning to look at her. She was so beautiful, so strong, so much better than me. "I'm so fucking scared, Lyd."

She wrapped an arm around my waist and said nothing. She didn't have to.

Reaching out with my mind I envisioned a hand at the end of arm unlatching and opening the heavy doors. As I saw it in my mind, it happened with no effort and no resistance. My father wanted to see me, he wasn't going to bar my path to him.

"Breathe," Lydia whispered in my ear.

I took in a long lungful of fresh mountain air.

"Who are you?" she asked.

"I am Alison Elizabeth Poole," I responded. My heartbeat, which had been racing started slowing down.

"What are you?" she pressed.

"I'm the Last Guardian of the Gate," I answered, the tremble leaving my voice replaced with an unnatural calmness.

"What do you have to do?" she asked.

"I have to walk down there and say hello to my father," I said. Then with a grin, I added, "Then I'm gonna tell him goodbye."

Lydia laughed.

I turned and wrapped my arms around her neck. She, in turn, slipped her other arm around my waist to join the other and we kissed.

I know I'm only sixteen, but you know when you have something amazing. This was the kind of kiss you see at the end of bad chick flicks and read about in bodice rippers. We were welded together at the lips, and it seemed the rest of our body parts were trying to join them.

"Wow," I whispered in a slurred voice when we reluctantly broke the kiss.

"You come back to me, and I'll show you 'Wow,'" she said laughing and crying simultaneously. It was a beautiful and heartbreaking image. I knew if I didn't come back from this insane mission I'd carry it in my heart forever.

"Okay, now it's really time," I said.

Lydia nodded unable to speak.

I turned to the now open doors and set a booted foot at the edge of the portal. The music increased, and the feeling of biting tinfoil filled my mouth followed by the rotten smell, causing my stomach to flip. This was it. Come Hell or high water only one person, or thing, would be coming back up those stairs. I stepped across the threshold and toward my fate.

The doors shut on their own behind me.

Chapter 22

"The Steps"

It was cold in the basement. Really cold. Like Hoth cold. The lights were turned on spilling their sickly fluorescent glow across the open space at the bottom of the stairs. Each of my breaths steamed and clouded into a dense fog in front of my eyes. Frost coated the beams and pillars supporting the house above.

Did I mention it was cold?

"I really should have dressed more appropriately," I muttered crossing my arms under my breasts and gripping my bare upper arms. "I think a tank-top and shorts were a bad choice as far as wardrobe goes when it comes to confronting the embodiment of evil. But my boots are totes wicked." I laughed nervously.

The music tried to cut through my mental defenses with renewed effort as I took each step down the stairs. Off key melodies overlapped and warred for dominance in my mind. The fillings in my lower molars vibrated in resonance with the tune. The result was intense pain spiderwebbing across my face. My knees went weak and a watery sensation, not unlike the first time I got drunk and puked all over the back porch, filled my lower half. Unable to remain upright I dropped with a thump to a sitting position on the steps, my knees pulled to my sweat soaked face.

"Stop!" I yelled both out loud and in my mind.

Silence, not as in all noise was banished from my hearing, but utter silence. At that moment I realized that even when my abilities were dormant, they still functioned on a basic level. I'd lived my life with a low almost comforting background buzz of thoughts and emotions from the people and animals around me. So integral was that haze of undefined mental activity that I never realized it was something everyone else lacked.

Until now.

Panic reared up at that moment and buried its claws in my mind and heart. There was no defined target of the fear, just a raw terror so intense I started sobbing before I knew the tears were coming. I wanted to run back up the half dozen steps and bang my hands on the doors begging to be let out. I knew I would pound, claw, and pummel the wood until my hands were nothing more than bloody stumps of raw meat and protruding white bone.

Music filled my head.

It wasn't the sickeningly, wrong alien music from beyond the door. That was well and truly banished for the moment. This music was different. This music was all too human. This music was something I remembered and loved.

When I was seven, I'd been staying here on the farm with Grandma and Grandpa and I'd gotten really sick. Step throat had transitioned to

Scarlatina and for a few days the local doctor had made house calls and debated sending me to the hospital in Charleston. In the end, my immune system had been stronger than the virus and I'd recovered after almost a month of bed rest. Most of that time is a blur to me but there was one moment on the third day I remember with perfect clarity.

It was dark, the middle of the night, and my family was taking shifts watching me. Grandpa Roy was sitting in the chair by my bed and for some reason he started singing. Not just any song, he sang my favorite song in the world. Sitting on that step, I heard it clear in my head as if I was back on the bed fighting off the virus that very much wanted to kill me.

"If you go down in the woods today, you're sure of a big surprise
If you go down in the woods today, you'd better go in disguise
For every bear that ever there was will gather there for certain
Because today's the day the teddy bears have their picnic."

Grandpa Roy's clear and surprisingly sweet voice filled my mind and I lifted my head from my shaking knees. There was nothing else, just the words and melody, and I closed my eyes and focused on them. In my mind, I could almost feel the covers wrapped around my small body and smell the vanilla from the candles my grandmother had lit in my bedroom.

"Every teddy bear who's been good is sure of a treat today
There's lots of marvelous things to eat and wonderful games to play
Beneath the trees where nobody sees, they'll hide and seek as long as
they please."

The fear, terror, panic and uncertainty melted from the places they'd settled in my body and drained away as the song continued. I remembered warm days and cool nights on the farm. Long, lazy Sundays with Grandpa Roy fixing something or caring for the animals. They were some of the happiest memories of my life.

"That's the way the teddy bears have their picnic."

This was my home. Even when I was little and lived hundreds of miles away, this had been the place my heart lived. My mother had left and thus abdicated her claim to the home place, and its mysteries, but me... I loved them all.

"Picnic time for teddy bears
The little teddy bears are having a lovely time today
Watch them, catch them unawares and see them picnic on their
holiday."

Shakily, like a toddler first learning the control their legs, and in some ways that was exactly what I was, I rose to my feet. My scuffed and heavy combat boots set firmly on the concrete riser of the steps. I stood at the center, above was the outside world and below was the thing. The thing behind the door.

"See them gaily gad about
They love to play and shout
They never have any cares
At six o'clock their mummies and daddies will take them back home to
bed
Because they're tired little teddy bears."

The fear was gone and in its place a rush of love and warmth filled me so intensely my heart lurched. Never in my life had I felt so whole, so complete, so loved. Was Grandpa Roy actually singing to me from the better place where he now resided? I don't know, but I'd like to think so. Just like with Daddy—I'd like to think he knew I needed him and he came. He came to me like he came to little Ally so many years before and sang joy back into my frightened heart.

"If you go down in the woods today, you better not go alone
It's lovely down in the woods today, but safer to stay at home
For every bear that ever there was will gather there for certain

Because today's the day the teddy bears have their picnic."

Strength joined the love as the song ended.

Was I still afraid? Yes, of course, somewhere in the back of my mind I was still afraid. I'd be an idiot not to be afraid. But now I knew that despite the closed doors and deafening silence, I wouldn't be doing this alone. I'd never really been alone.

With no more hesitation I descended the stairs and planted my feet on the smooth stone of the basement floor. In front of me was the door. The door that was and was not in the basement, stood wide open. A sickly green-yellow, and dirty white light pulsated in the opening.

"This is my house," I said, clenching my fists at my sides, my voice cutting the preternatural silence. "This is my house and I want you out."

The light beckoned me forward. I could almost hear it laughing at me, taunting from the other side.

Anger, no let's be honest, white hot rage filled my blood.

"All right Dad," I hissed. "Fuck you, we'll do it the hard way."

Never breaking step I marched through the open door.

It closed behind me.

Chapter 23

"Hello Father"

I expected pain.

I expected terror.

I expected gut-churning vertigo.

Fuck, I expected to feel some discomfort when I crossed the threshold. Instead, there was just quiet and darkness. And if I'm going to be honest, the darkness was pleasant. Not the cold, unrelenting darkness, but the warm and peaceful tranquility of an afternoon nap on a cool autumn day.

"Look at you," a voice said from the darkness. "Strong, tall, and beautiful. Credit to your species, one such as you, my daughter, has not tread this world in ten thousand years." The voice of my father was even more pleasant than the darkness. The sonorous almost melodic tones soothed me.

The darkness changed but did not disappear. The black morphed and swirled like ink flowing from a bottle to be replaced by a lush blue and indigo swirl. Yellow and red stars filled the new sky, and a firmament of purple grass grew beneath my feet. Large trees of many shapes topped with pale pink leaves encircled the clearing we stood in. Unseen animals scurried through the underbrush while large semitransparent creatures glided soundlessly through the sky.

From the retreating black, a figure coalesced.

"Hello Alison," my other father said. "Welcome home."

He was tall but not enormous. My real father was taller. His skin was so pale I wondered for a second if he was a clown wearing makeup, of course he was not, but the in the dimness of the environment the white was striking. Short coal black hair topped his head and bright yellow eyes filled out the appearance.

He was, in his own terrifying way, beautiful.

"Do you like my home?" he asked gesturing with a white hand tipped with delicate black claws. "Once, long before the speaking of the word and my banishment, all the universe looked thus."

I imagined the primitive life of the primordial world living in the perpetual twilight and shivered. But part of me yearned to remain forever within the darkness. There was an innocence and safety in it.

"But once my sibling made his decision," he brought his hand down, and the sky exploded with light. "All that ended."

The pale stars were banished by a bright white sun, not the sun that warms the Earth but one far older. The purple grass withered and browned under the glare of the orb to be replaced by bright green shoots. The creatures in the air and amongst the burning trees shrieked in fear and agony. Then they were silent.

"Did he care that I loved what I'd made? Of course not, all he cared about were his creations," my father spat.

"What do you want?" I asked, finally finding my voice. "Why are you showing me all of this?"

"Call it a preview of things to come," he responded taking a step forward.

I instinctively took a step backwards.

"I mean you no harm, Alison," he said pausing and raising a placating, taloned hand. "If I wanted you dead you'd already be dead."

That was when I felt that tickle in the back of mind. He was telling the truth, but he was lying as well. I knew this well as I knew my family loved me and that Lydia was the best kisser I'd ever met. But I was not able to determine what the truths and the lies were.

"If you mean me no harm then why did you try to take me when I was a child?" I asked.

"Does a father not have a right to know his child?" he responded taking another step forward.

This time, I braced my feet and remained still. I wasn't going to give ground to this thing. Instead, I replied almost laughing, "I have a father, and you are not him."

"You have no concept of what you are," he purred icily.

His eyes locked with mine and flashed with an inner fire filling my mind with scenes and images. I saw many worlds, all different from one another and yet the same. They were all Earth and the same time as were all separate worlds. Some were from the far past and others the future, but each shared one thing. In each of those words my father,

Ast-Murath whose name I now knew translated to The Maker, was at this moment active and trying to escape his confinement.

On one world it was the far future and the Earth was a wrecked mess filled with magic and superscience. I watched as my father attempted to escape his prison only to be stopped by an achingly beautiful woman with a mighty hammer. In another vision, I saw the world overrun by the living dead and my father using a lost portal and ancient human magic to escape only to be stopped by a woman and young man, the door to his realm shut from that world for ten thousand years. There were other worlds, too many to count where I watched his attempts to escape thwarted again and again.

With an effort, I broke the connection between us.

"Too long I've suffered here in my confinement," he murmured, a new bitterness filling his voice. "But now… now I have a chance. Now we have a chance, Alison."

"A chance for what?" I asked already starting to put the pieces together in my mind. The reason he'd never really hurt me, why he'd taken my mother and planted his seed, and most importantly why in all those other realities he'd thus far failed, but now he was sure he could succeeded.

His features grew dim and the blackness I'd first been greeted with returned. Now there was none of the comfort and warmth from before, instead cold fear filled the space.

I shivered and once more wished for a coat.

"When you leave this place Alsion you will no longer be alone," he said, his body if it'd ever been a body, dissolved into the inky blackness. "We will be one, and together we will tear down the pillars of creation and lay waste to the wreckage!"

On his last word the blackness launched toward me and enveloped my body.

Chapter 24

"The Dark Side"

I saw it all from above.

The moon hung in the sky above me broken into a multitude of pieces and spread across the sky in a broad streak. The sky itself was an inky black blotting out the stars and seemed to be pressing down on the Earth. An Earth that was scorched and cracked. The skeletons of dead trees dotted the landscape and basins, which once held lakes and seas, sat dry and barren. The bones of dead cities and the broken works of the human race dotted the surface of the dead world.

But life was not completely stripped from the world of my birth. Tribes of degenerate and primitive humans clustered in few areas still capable of sustaining life. In these places, they offered human sacrifices on altars of obsidian before cyclopean statues of a single creature, a woman of terrible beauty.

Statues of me.

"What is this?" I whispered as horror filled my heart.

"This, Alison," my father spoke in my mind, "is just the beginning of what we will accomplish once we leave my prison. Look at it, look at the beauty of the destruction."

I wanted to scream for him to stop but a small part of me, a part I never knew lived in my heart, looked at the spectacle and loved it. A dark, sinister spark buried deep in my core yearned to revel in the potential death and chaos I was being shown. It wanted the worship of these savages.

"The power calls to you Alis-Murath," my father purred in my mind.

"That's not my name!" I hissed breaking my gaze from the infernal blood rites being performed across the dead world.

"Yes it is," he assured me. "It's the name I placed on your heart at your conception."

"I don't want any of this," I said thickly, my eyes returning to the surface of the planet by their own volition.

"You can't lie to me Alis-Murath," he answered silkily. "I can see the darkness in your soul. It's part of me."

Invisible cold hands gripped my shoulders, and the vision of the dead Earth under me and my father's dominion swirled and became a muddy blotch of color. Once more we were in the black void.

But in the blink between realities, there'd been something else.

"Time means nothing here child, we have an eternity for you to accept your destiny. Once you do, we'll cross the threshold together, and it will be as if a moment has passed." He grinned as he spoke, his eyes glowing brightly.

I was only partially paying attention to his proclamations. There'd been something in that hundredth of a heartbeat. Something so big it dwarfed everything my father had shown me. But I couldn't clarify it in my mind. It was important—I knew that much, I also knew my father had no idea it'd been there.

"We will bring the humans to heel and when the so-called Great Old Ones rise to stop us we will make them our dogs!" He was building up a real head of steam and not really talking to me anymore.

I pressed my powers as hard as I could. I needed to know what I'd seen in that moment.

"Even Cthulhu and Lucifer will bow before me and do my bidding!" he raged into infinite darkness, his skin smoking in response to his rage.

My skull felt as it would split open and rivulets of blood would run from my ears, nose, and the corners of my eyes. I dropped to my knees smashing my hands to the sides of my head and screaming silently into the void.

"Then we will find my sibling and root him out of his hidy-hole!"

Then I had it. In an instant of perfect clarity, I saw the vision in its entirety.

Earth, many years from now. The moon was whole, the air was clean, and the world had a feeling of hope and potential. I saw myself walking through a park. I was an adult, fully formed and as my gran used to say, "Done cooking" and I looked good although I walked with the aid of a slender cane for some reason. Lydia walked next to me, and we were holding hands, but that wasn't the most wonderful part. That would be the stroller she was pushing with her free hand. Nestled inside and sound asleep was our son. Then it happened. He reached out to me with his mind.

I don't mean the little boy of barely six months reached out to the me in the vision, I mean he reached out to the real me. The me who'd walked through the doorway. He wasn't a possible person he was already real, somewhere in the quantum foam of the universe, my son already lived and he wanted to be born. The love within and the joy of his touch ignited an inferno in me. In the instant of our contact and his wordless emotions, I knew love, desire, and destiny like I'd never imagined possible.

"I want that," I whispered.

"What?!" my father snapped, his monolog broken.

"You wanted me to sacrifice my son without even knowing I was doing it," I said rising to my shaky legs.

"How do you—" he started to ask but I never let him finish.

The fire, the love, the anger, the hurt, and the fear catalyzed within me, and I screamed.

Power is a funny thing. I don't mean funny like a clown being run over by an ice cream truck because seriously fuck all clowns, but funny like a single dry area in the middle of a thunderstorm. Objectively Daddy Dearest should've been able to wipe the floor with me—at best I had half his power. But at that moment, that one single confluence of time, space, and chance I got the drop on him. So fixated was he on his plan that the idea a sixteen year old girl, even one of my power, could stand against him was inconceivable.

And yes I know how to use that word.

Were you expecting a big throw down between myself and thing that sired me? Sorry, that's not how these things end—stories like mine are always a little anticlimactic. He'd had his chance to tempt me and if I'm going to be honest, and why would I start lying to you now, he almost won. I knew that if I was alive a hundred years from now, I'd still feel that pull.

So what happened?

I screamed and the power I unleashed blasted Ast-Murath, The Maker, across a hundred realities.

Then I ran.

That's right kids, I ran for dear life before Daddy Dearest could gain his footing and come after me. His powers might be throttled in his prison, but they were more than enough to force his way into me no matter how much I fought him. He wanted me to willingly let him in, but in a pinch, he'd take what he wanted, just like he did to Mom.

"Get back here you bitch!" he screamed from far away, but I knew he was closing fast.

The door back to the basement, back to my world, was a speck in the distance far ahead of me.

"We could have done this the easy way," he snarled his voice closer. "But no, like all the talking monkeys you have to be difficult!"

The terror was back. I'd refused him. I'd surprised him. And to a limited degree, I'd done something few had ever done in the past—I'd scared him.

"You could've had it all Alison, but now you'll just be the vessel I ride out of this hell!"

I could feel his breath on the nape of my neck. The door handle was clear and bright, a beacon of the living world drawing me forward.

"You can't escape me!" he raged, his voice now monstrous. More that of a snarling animal than a thinking creature.

I felt the tips of his taloned hands slice deep into my back at the same moment my hand gripped the handle. Pain exploded through my body and light flashed brightly from the door. The last thing I heard was my father's guttural animal screams before I stepped through the doorway.

Chapter 25

"Closure"

Standing on the threshold between my father's prison and the world of my birth, I realized I was well and truly fucked. The door between words was open and even though I was able to keep Ast-Murath out of my mind, he had his claws figuratively and literally embedded in me. Pain ripped through my body, and I was pretty sure my spine might have been severed. I had the power to pull myself through the doorway and back into the real world but if I did that I'd drag my father along with me.

And he knew it.

"Turn around and face your destiny," he whispered. "Or step through the doorway and clear the path for me. Either way, my time is now, and the worlds will burn in my wake."

"I will never let you out!" I hissed my body above the waist racked with agony. I wasn't positive how I was still standing in the doorway considering my useless legs, but I was sure it had something to do with my abilities and the nature of the portal.

"How long can you stand between worlds?" he cooed. "How long can you maintain your position with your crippled body? I do not need you to exit the portal whole, Alis-Murath, just alive."

"That is not my name!" I screamed with my mouth and my mind.

There was no finesse to my attack. I hadn't been cognizant of my gifts for long and I'd had almost zero time to prepare for this. But maybe that was a good thing. If I'd been aware in front of my mind just how outclassed I was, I might've curled up and surrendered to his power. Instead, I harnessed my rage and fear for one last attack emptying my power onto him like a thunderstorm.

Ast-Murath, my father, the thing that'd taken my mother against her will and left me behind like a dark and putrid Easter egg withdrew screaming in shock and I like to believe fear.

He was gone, but I was spent. I collapsed onto the threshold still stuck between worlds my useless legs unable to move me and with no power left to compensate. I had to get out before he returned. The door between worlds had to be shut and locked for another ten thousand years.

Help me! I called with my mind.

The coven was gathered outside the entrance to the basement. They were there to do one thing. They were there to be my lifeline if I needed one. I sure as hell needed one now. At first, I didn't think they could hear me. I was sure my father was blocking the connection between me and the coven. And maybe he was, but there was one connection he had no chance of breaking.

We're here baby, Mom replied in my mind

Tendrils of warmth encircled my body in a loose comforting web of thought.

"No!" Ast-Murath screamed, and I could feel him bounding towards me and the portal to the real world.

There was nothing I could do. I put all of my faith in my family new and old.

Each tendril tugged at my body in an uncoordinated tangle of motion. I was afraid they wouldn't be able to work in unison enough to save me. I was able to see the glow of my father's eyes growing larger as he chewed up the distance between us.

Now would be great! I yelled with the last bit of mental power I had left.

More than a dozen mental hands solidified into one and jerked me through the doorway like a rag doll on a string. The door slammed shut and faded from existence as I was pulled up the stairs and into the light of the day.

I thought for a moment I heard my father scream one last time.

I landed flat on my back as the bulkhead doors slammed shut.

The quiet was overwhelming in its simplicity. I thought I could still hear the otherworldly music building to its terrifying crescendo one last time, but I knew in my bones it was just an echo in my mind. Everything was black, and I was horrified for a moment believing my eyes had been burned out of my skull in my final confrontation with my father. I was ready to scream and let the panic overtake me when I realized my eyes were shut.

"Ally?" a voice asked. It sounded far away, and like I heard it from several feet under water. But it was still a voice I'd have known anywhere.

"Lydia?" I asked my voice choked and my tongue heavy in my mouth.

Arms wrapped around and lifted my body from the ground.

"Ouch!" I hissed when pain radiated from the deep gashes on my back.

"Allison are you okay?" Mom asked.

I opened my eyes and saw the entirety of the Moon Dust Coven gathered around me in a circle. Mom and Lydia knelt by me, and of course, Lydia was the one with her arms around me. Everyone looked shell shocked, and I can't say I blamed them.

"My back," I groaned.

Slowly Mom and Lydia turned me over to reveal the shredded shirt and deep cauterized gouges in my flesh. I heard Lydia gasp and Mom begin to weep.

"My legs," I added tears leaking from my own eyes.

"What about them?" Mom asked, her eyes scanning my seemingly undamaged lower appendages. "They look alright to me."

"I can't feel them," I sobbed then added. "He broke my spine."

Lydia was the first to react to that news pulling her forehead to mine until we touched. Our minds and hearts mingled, and all I felt was love. My maiming meant nothing to her, and she wanted me to know.

"You're alive," Mom said, squeezing my hand so hard I winced. She eased her grip and added, "You saved the world Ally, you saved us all."

I looked up, the sun was still high in the sky, and the air still smelled of apples and lilacs.

Everything was right with the world.

ABOUT THE AUTHOR

When I was born on August 3, 1976, in the great state of Michigan the hills shook and the sky was swept with fire. These were portents of the greatness for my future that was written in the stars ... I'm still waiting for that greatness.

My name is Josh Hilden, and I am many things. I am a husband, father, a son, a friend. These are all important things but at my core I am an artist and the medium that I work in is words. I am a writer of Role Playing Games, short stories, essays, poetry, novellas, and novels.

In the everyday world, I can be found spending time with my family and friends. I have been married to my lovely wife Karen since September of 1996. We have six amazing children. We tend to be a family of unabashed geeks and gamers who were geek before geek was chic.

If you are interested in me, I am very active online with a personal and a writing blog along with a plethora of social media outlets. All links are available on my website (www.joshhilden.com). If you have any questions or just want to chat hit me up!

E-Mail: josh@joshhilden.com

www.joshhilden.com

Amazon US:

https://www.amazon.com/s/ref=nb_sb_noss?url=search-alias%3Dstripbooks&field-keywords=gws+press&rh=n%3A283155%2Ck%3Agws+press

Amazon UK:

https://www.amazon.co.uk/s/ref=nb_sb_noss?url=search-alias%3Dstripbooks&field-keywords=GWS+Press

Amazon CA:

https://www.amazon.ca/s/ref=nb_sb_noss/166-9929103-9487132?url=search-alias%3Dstripbooks&field-keywords=GWS+Press

Amazon AU:

https://www.amazon.com.au/s/ref=nb_sb_noss/352-0412353-3786030?url=search-alias%3Ddigital-text&field-keywords=GWS+Press

A Call to Action
aka
How to Help An Indie Writer

We are Indie Writers. This means that we either self-publishing our work or we are being published by a small company and not one of the "Big 6" publishers. We enjoy being independent; we can write what we want when we want with little to no oversight from above. It also means we are doing all of the heavy lifting for ourselves, and that is the part we enjoy the least. We don't enjoy constantly spamming social media with information on our latest works, but it's a task we have to do.

"What can I do to help you out?" you ask.

The answer is very simple. There is a short list of things you can do to give us a helping hand.

•Share information about our work with your friends and family

•Like, review, and rate our work wherever and whenever you can.

•Finally, you can sign up for the company mailing list (link below) to keep up with the latest goings-on our work

We at **Gorillas With Scissors Press** look forward to producing more products that you can enjoy, and we anticipate a long and happy reader/writer relationship!

Subscribe to the Josh Hilden Mailing List

http://eepurl.com/bKrXjH

Support Me on Patreon

Do you like helping? Do you like free books and awesome swag? Do you like getting free books and awesome swag for helping?

If you answered yes to any of that, perhaps you would like support me on Patreon so I can to continue producing genre fiction without dealing with the standard gate keepers and barriers in the publishing industry.

But what do you get out of it?

What, helping me out isn't enough? Well, I agree the good feeling of helping isn't enough. Depending on your subscription amount members get access to content beyond the Pay Wall, monthly Skype or Google Hangout Q&A's, exclusive behind the scenes information, a monthly (or more often) exclusive story, free digital copies of my new releases, free paperbacks, free audio-books, when new swag is created (buttons, stickers, bookmarks..., etc.) Patreon members get the first crack.

What will I do with these funds?

First and foremost, I'll be hiring new freelance staff. I am in desperate need of a full-time copy editor/proofreader along with an art director. After that, we'll be using the funds for more promotional/marketing spending.

I hope you choose to join me on this journey of growth and expansion!

https://www.patreon.com/joshhilden

- Josh Hilden

Printed in Great Britain
by Amazon

21592404R00078